The Practice, the Horizon, and the Chain

ALSO BY SOFIA SAMATAR

A Stranger in Olondria
The Winged Histories
Tender: Stories
Monster Portraits (with Del Samatar)
The White Mosque: A Memoir
Tone (with Kate Zambreno)

THE
PRACTICE,
THE
HORIZON,
AND
THE CHAIN

SOFIA SAMATAR

TOR PUBLISHING GROUP
NEW YORK

THE PRACTICE, THE HORIZON, AND THE CHAIN

Copyright © 2024 by Sofia Samatar

Cover design by Jamie Stafford-Hill

A Tordotcom Book
Published by Tom Doherty Associates / Tor Publishing Group
120 Broadway
New York, NY 10271

www.tor.com

Tor® is a registered trademark of Macmillan Publishing Group, LLC.

ISBN 978-1-250-88181-6 (ebook)
ISBN 978-1-250-88180-9 (trade paperback)

First Edition: 2024

*For my teachers
and my students*

The Practice, the Horizon, and the Chain

1

The Practice

THE BOY WAS TAKEN UPSTAIRS without warning, un-protesting as he had been through all the changes in his seventeen years, the shifts from cell to cell each time he outgrew the bolt on his ankle and the Doctor came to exchange it for a larger one, an operation performed with a tool the Hold people called the Mallet, which jarred the whole leg and sometimes made the blood spray from the anklebone, and caused a sense of queasiness and superstitious awe in the boy, who would glimpse, for the instant during which the bolt and chain were removed, the shiny and alien-looking patch of underexposed skin on his leg which, according to the prophet, housed the seat of the soul.

The changes had taken the boy to different cells in the Hold and attached him to sundry gangs and a variety of labors, crawling or climbing, lifting or mucking out or pounding repetitively, but always the basic routines and rituals remained the same, the pap and drink served at the same hours, the negotiations with others carried out according to a precise set of regulations: you did not toss and turn at night so as not to yank the others awake, you held your insides tight until it was time to use the jakes, if a man was sick you gathered with others to truss him in the chains and carried your part of the extra burden without complaint. Like others he had experimented with fighting, learning to use the chain that bound them together to whip or trip his opponent, the older men watching until they decided it had gone far enough and took up the chains to haul the combatants apart. Like others he had celebrated on feast days, when they were given an extra drink, and taken part in the complex chain dancing. On rest days he played a game of Pick or Scatter. He had been put in the Meet Rooms and, through good fortune, managed to talk to the same girl twice.

His life had been so ordinary that going upstairs in the lift, that brilliant box of light whose rays seemed to pierce his head from every direction, with its violently compressed air that made him sink down and sit on the floor among the guards who stood there smiling as if their bellies were not being squashed into pap, he could think of only two reasons why he should be singled out and torn from his kin in this way: the pictures, and the prophet.

He was not the only one to make pictures. The walls of the cells were scored with them. He used to carve them with a bit of castoff: a bent nail or a broken lid from the bins. The chain itself could be used for rubbing, creating effects of texture and depth. It was noisy work and dull for others and often he had been scolded for it in childhood, but this had changed in the past few years, when he had shared his cell with the prophet, who told the others to leave the boy alone and taught him to bargain for time, to make deals with the rest of the gang that allowed him to draw. The prophet told the boy that his passion for drawing was a gift that must be handled with great care, for it was as precious as breathing. The prophet's own gift was language, and the boy saw how he had honed it and kept it bright and made it a thing of value for others as well as himself. He saw how people listened to the prophet, how on feast days, when the guards with their buzzing blue anklets came to unlock the chain at the door, when all the gangs were led out and latched to the walls of the vast, cold hangar for a few hours, the prophet's voice could command the whole crowd. He was a little old man with gleaming skin and a belly rounded by the extra pap and drinks he was given as gifts. His voice did not carry far and so when he spoke a whispering filled the hangar, hundreds of mouths passing on what he had said. He spoke of the Wilderness and the River of Life. He spoke of the Wheel in the Middle of the Air and the Valley where the Bones lay sleeping.

He spoke of the Star called Wormwood that makes the waters bitter, and afterward the boy put these things into some of his pictures. Under the tutelage of the prophet, he began both to work out agreements that let him go on with his drawings and to make pictures of greater ambition and scope, scenes that incorporated the older work of unknown artists into visions fraught with increasing beauty and terror.

When the Doctor came to remove him from that cell, where his pictures were, he began to cry, and the prophet told him to watch, to always watch and seek for the River of Life. "How will I know it?" the boy asked, and the prophet told him, "It's the River that is a Sea."

The boy had never seen either river or sea. "I don't understand," he said, and the prophet said sadly that he himself was as ignorant as the boy, that he possessed nothing but bones and a chain and a wish to touch the truth. This longing for awareness he called the Practice.

Now going up in the lift the boy remembered the prophet's words and how the Doctor had turned for a moment to look at the old man in bemusement, turning just for a breath before he called the next in line to go under the Mallet, sending a single appraising glance toward the soft old prophet, a glance which, the boy now realized, had also taken in his own tearstained face and the pictures that covered the walls of the cell—a glance which, he thought in his misery, had contained something small, intent, and dangerous, like a spark in the deepest wires of the Ship.

~

The woman woke to the crackling of her anklet and knew the boy had come upstairs. She leaned toward her clock: the numbers glowed *06:00*. The stars outside the window were growing pale. She would not sleep again now. She turned off the alarm, switched on the light, and headed for the shower.

As the steam poured around her she thought of the boy who had come upstairs for the first time, wearing the angular bolt with six feet of chain attached, a chain that had hampered his movements his whole life, locked to other chains or a wall. She thought of her father, who had grown up in the same way. Her father, too, had been selected to come up from the Hold, to be educated. He had become a professor of the Newer Knowledge. Every evening when she was growing up, he had consumed a single small glass of Hold water, which he ordered specially from the Commissary. The woman's mother had not been raised in the Hold; she came from a long line of guards and had always worn the blue circlet on her ankle, and she cringed at her husband's predilection for drinking the water of his childhood, which was only fit, she said, for flushing and irrigation. "It'll give you worms," she warned. But the woman, drying her hair, remembered the gentleness of her father's face, his whole body, while he drank, a relaxation and quietude that came over him as the lighting system dimmed, enveloping the Ship in a violaceous twilight. He had let her sip the water; she made a face. "Tastes like soap." As she dressed, she decided to order some of this water for the boy, who was no doubt frightened by the strangeness of his new world, and might be comforted by the brackish taste of home.

The woman was a professor of the Older Knowledge. She could say this, at last, after a decade-long struggle with the University, which had always divided the Knowledges into "Old" and "New"—an insulting categorization, complained the professors of what had then been called the Old Knowledge, which made their discipline appear quaint and useless, affecting their student numbers, always lower than those in the so-called Department of the New Knowledge, and limited their access to space and funding. The woman had led the task force to change the department names. She had made an impassioned speech—a speech that, said her friend Gil, who worked with her on the task force, had played a key role in changing the opinion of the Board—in which she defended the value of the arts. "My father taught the skills we need to survive in the vastness of space," she had said. "I teach the skills we need to *humanize* space." She had spoken of the power of public parks and the marvelous beauty of the songs of the chain gangs, which her father had sung to her. The task force had been successful, the names changed—not, as the woman had wished, to the Department of Arts and the Department of Sciences, but still, the shift from *Old* to *Older* Knowledge was an improvement, and to get those arrogant windbags on the other side of the bridge to call themselves *Newer*, rather than *New*, was nothing less than a coup, said Gil. The woman had received a Unity Award for Excellence in Service and, riding the wave of her achievements, had entered into another long battle, in which she was also victorious, and revived the University Scholarship for the Chained.

The scholarship program, briefly fashionable a generation ago, had brought several gifted young people up from the Hold, including the woman's father, but had decayed over the years due to lack of interest and funding, leaving the Hold, as the woman had argued to the Board, "a blank beneath our feet." But that time was about to end. The link between the upper and lower worlds was being reforged. Buttoning her shirt, the woman felt a brief tug of pain, a longing for her father to be alive again, for his whole generation, lost now to time, who would have known how to talk to the boy. *But I'll have to do it,* she thought. *I'm the best he's got.*

Gil met her at the café, as planned. He had already bought her a coffee. "He's here," he said, his eyes bright with excitement. "I just checked." He slipped his phone into his pocket. He never liked to use it in front of the woman, a sensitivity she appreciated.

She did not tell him that she already knew the boy was here, from the feel of her anklet, the slight twinge that meant a new link had been connected. She never spoke to him of the anklet, nor did he ask about it.

"Is Marjorie coming?" she asked, sipping her coffee.

"On her way."

The woman suppressed her annoyance at Marjorie's lateness. Marjorie, she knew, was simply one of those people you had to deal with in life: a colleague who clung to original projects like grit but hardly ever contributed except to make irritating objections at crucial moments, who wanted a share of success without working for it (thought the woman) or (said Gil) might actually be reporting to the administration, and was probably (they agreed) responsible for the line in the woman's last review that had called her "hard to work with and occasionally overbearing."

Marjorie arrived, dragging her feet, with her usual aggrieved expression. "It's so early," she said.

Gil said he'd ordered the wheelchair; it would be there soon, sent over by Gil's cousin, a Doctor who worked in the Hold, the one who had noticed the boy and his talent for drawing.

As they walked down to the security station, a crow skimmed over the street. *He's never seen a bird,* the woman thought.

"Maybe you should go in first, alone," Gil suggested to the woman. "It might be more comfortable for him."

"I don't see why," said Marjorie.

"Yes," said the woman firmly. "You're right, Gil." *Go ahead, call me overbearing,* she thought.

"Anything you want us to do while we're waiting?" asked Gil.

"Yes, actually," said the woman. "Could you have the Commissary send us some Hold water?"

"Some what?" said Marjorie.

"Hold water. It's what they drink—down there."

"They have their own water?"

"Sure," said Gil. "Happy to."

The woman gave him a grateful look.

Marjorie pulled out her phone, and the glances exchanged between Gil and the woman took on a rueful cast. "I could have slept in," muttered Marjorie, punching numbers.

The woman entered the station alone. "Hey, sis," said

the guard. "You're here for the chainey? He's in there. His lucky day."

~

The boy sat curled against the wall, pressing his cheek to the eerily wet and pallid surface that seemed to cling to his skin but which was yet recognizable as *wall,* as some sort of support. He breathed. He listened to the air going in and out of his lips, his throat. That was the Practice, the prophet had said. It was one form of the Practice, breathing and listening. The boy breathed through his mouth, trying not to smell the stinging air, the stench of the hard new clothes he wore and the shower where they had shaved him all over then boiled him so he thought he was going to die. But they hadn't killed him. They had done something worse. He couldn't move. He breathed at the wall. If he pulled away from it the whole room jumped and rippled. He couldn't look down at his legs. Even to think of it made him shake. They had taken his chain away and turned him into a guard.

Water came into his mouth. He was a guard, a blueleg. He remembered listening to stories in the Hold. How once there was a blueleg witch who came down the corridors making a little wheedling noise, *Blueleg blueleg will you trim my sail,* and anybody she touched with her pale blue finger would have to follow her forever, their eyes turned up and white, their hands flapping horribly, striving to clear away a foam that nobody else could see, that invaded their eyes and their heads and made them blue-leg too.

Another swell of water filled his mouth. He swallowed gingerly. He could hear the little keening whine that was himself.

A guard came in and spoke to him. The boy moved his eyes to see her but not his face, because he couldn't leave the wall. She was telling him to get up and sit in the chair. He knew he could not. Instead he closed his eyes and waited for the truncheon.

And maybe if I'm no good as a guard they'll send me back, he thought.

But the truncheon did not fall. The guard went away and came back with a drink of water. She crouched beside him and held it to his face and he drank a little, then stopped because it wasn't going to stay down. He kept his eyes on the floor, trying hopelessly to avoid smelling the guard-smell that was the odor of himself, waiting in a confused agony of terror for her to tell him what was going to happen next, what he must do.

"Look at me," she said. He moved his eyes to her.

She spoke to him quietly, as he had heard no guard speak before. The sound prickled down his neck. *She is the blueleg witch,* he thought, his mind whirling with horror so he could hardly hear what she said. All he understood was that he would have to try the chair. She took his arm. "There," she said.

When he left the wall, the room flipped over. He groaned and sprawled, crushed down like a louse in the huge light of the room that swung in violent circles around his body.

He threw up a little water on the floor.

"Hey," said the witch-guard. "You're all right."

"I can't see," gasped the boy. The world was blotted out. There was only a baleful nebulous pulsing grayness of malignant light in which he flailed witlessly, seeking some kind of purchase. The foam was in his head now and he must tread in her wake forever. His hand flew up and hit something. Then she took his arm again and there was direction. With her help, he managed to sit in the chair, and she sat beside him holding his hand, patting it and telling him he had done well.

Slowly his vision returned and he looked at her. Her eye was red and with a cold pang in his belly he realized he had struck her. "It's nothing, it's nothing," she said, squeezing his hand. She told him in her witchy nonguard voice that her father had been like him, a boy from the Hold, that he had told her the first twenty-four hours after the chain came off were the worst, that soon, very soon, the boy would be able to walk again. "It's because you've grown used to the tension of the chain," she said. "You're not used to walking alone, to sensing anything by yourself." She said it would be easier if he could think about his new anklet as a kind of chain, one that bound him to others, just in a different way.

"You might not notice it yet," she said, "but there are little changes in the buzz. You can tell when a person joins, when a dying person leaves. With time, you can even sense distance. I can feel, for example, that there are twelve of us here in this security station."

She smiled while he fought to breathe through the abominable twitching blue circle that ringed his soul.

She said many other things. She talked to him about drawing, about the pictures he had made on the walls, and tears came into his eyes at this confirmation of the reason for his punishment. He wanted to run downstairs and scratch out every picture he'd ever made: the picture of the drowned men, of the stars, of the prophet and his child. But he couldn't move. He couldn't sit up if she took her hand away. Keeping hold of his wrist, she gave him a little more water. A few drops fell on his shirt and rolled right off the shiny fabric. She said he would be all right. She said he should call her "professor." In that void of dead light she asked if he had any questions, and though he knew himself lost beyond hope of deliverance, he said,

"Can I have my chain back?"

~

The woman and Gil and Marjorie took the boy to his new room in the dormitory. The boy sat with his head on his knees, only raising himself when the wheelchair had stopped moving, and he barely touched the food and drink laid out for him under the colorful Welcome sign. The students from Gil's sociology class, who had brought the food and decorated the room, were there to receive their new colleague, as well as the professors who had helped create the scholarship, several representatives from student organizations, the head of the Campus Committee for Unity and Multiplicity, and the members of the Faculty, Staff, and Student Ankleted Alliance, known informally as the Ring. Even President Lyle stopped by and shook the boy's hand. The room grew hot and crowded. People leaned down to catch the boy's words, asking him to repeat himself as he answered their questions in the soft, rounded accent that reminded the woman of her father.

"I hope this isn't too much for him," she remarked to her colleague Angela, who had worked with her on the scholarship committee.

"Poor thing," Angela sighed, scraping the last icing

from her plate. "But he's all right for now. It's being alone that will bother him. They're not used to it."

Angela, an anthropologist, specialized in chained behaviors. She had spoken fervently to the Board in support of the scholarship, stressing the need for understanding across the human spectrum, and winning a burst of enthusiastic applause. At the time, the woman had regarded Angela's speech as effective but distasteful: Angela came from an old mining family, her uncle sat on the Board, and her whole upbringing had been removed from the idea of the Hold, so while her action on behalf of the scholarship was necessary to its success, there was something exaggerated, the woman felt, in her humid eyes and distraught gestures. But now the woman saw that Angela had guessed at the boy's feelings in a way she herself had not. Her face burned; she felt she ought to have anticipated the boy's needs without being told.

At last everyone was gone except the members of the Ring, their blue anklets adding a subtle silvery tone to the atmosphere. They cleaned up the room and packed the leftover food away in the boy's refrigerator and took down the Welcome sign. The woman felt an ease and elasticity in the air, familiar to her from childhood, when her parents' friends would gather in the evening, playing cards or singing, resting their stocking feet on the coffee table while a cool thread, fragile and soothing, came into the buzz of the anklets. She hoped the boy could feel it: the closeness of the circle in the room, the care. She saw one of the older faculty, whom she thought of as her elders, lay a hand briefly on the boy's head while taking up his plate. The boy sat very still; at least he did not flinch.

The oldest among them, the humble elder, a tall, stooped man worn fine as a clean, well-used rag by his years of service, so that the mildness of his temperament shone through all his looks and gestures, took the boy away to explain the toilet and shower. The woman stood by the window; she could hear the students of the Ring in the courtyard below, dumping the trash from the party in the bins. Their casual laughter made her throat tighten. They would be the ones, she knew, to embrace and shield the boy. They would help him absorb the insult of being taught about himself in Angela's anthropology class, they would rally around him silently in Raymond's history class (notorious in the Ring for promoting rigid notions of human destiny), they would suffer with him in sympathy through the regimental program of Alvin's drawing class, they would teach him to slap hands with them in Gil's sociology class, to plaster protest signs around the cafeteria, to paint skulls on the dormitory steps. And the elders would be there, too, as they had been there for the woman herself, to guide him, watch over him, and rescue him. One of these, the jaded elder, approached the woman where she stood at the window and smiled, arms crossed, head shaking. "I didn't think you could pull it off."

The jaded elder was nearly the same age as the humble elder—both had been close friends of the woman's father—but while the humble elder had risen to a high administrative position, the jaded elder, due to her uncompromising character, had been passed over for promotions and slowly forced from a role of importance, and even from the public eye, into a back office with a broken heater. She had a great many tasks that "*somehow,*" she would say with her throaty, explosive laugh, "never add up to anything," and could be seen riding to work on an aged scooter early in the morning, wrapped up in scarves to face the biting chill of her workspace.

Now she eyed the woman keenly. "You need to get some sleep."

"I know. But I thought I'd sit out in the hall. In case he needs something in the night."

"You'll burn yourself out," the jaded elder told her, and the woman knew she was right, but she couldn't leave. When the humble elder had tucked the boy into bed, when the boy was lying there flat on his back looking up at the ceiling, his eyes unmoving, his hands on top of the blankets pressed down stiffly at his sides, when everyone else had gone away, she told the boy she would stay outside the door. "I can leave it open a crack, if you want."

He didn't respond.

"Do you want me to prop the door open a little?"

"Yes."

"Should I leave the light on?"

"No."

She sat outside. Gradually the dormitory grew silent. The boy made no sound in the night and in the morning she found him under the bed, with no blanket or pillow, pressed back against the wall.

~

So he had come upstairs into blueleg country. It was a country of damp air. He felt the air push into his lungs, he felt himself breathing, walking as he was bidden along the pavements beneath the enormous dome of sky where the heaviness of the air collected in a fine mist. Beside the pavements, networks of water trickled in glistening tubes. The walls sweated. The rooms where the boy was sent had luminous deep-green windows, where algae thickened between the double panes. The glass was warm to the touch. The water they gave him to drink there tasted sweet.

He was sent into different rooms and given objects to hold and manipulate and presented with a dizzying variety of foods. Bleak and dogged he made his way, always feeling that he was somehow walking sideways, or as if everything around him hung at an angle. The light upstairs was hot, immense, and ruthless. He noticed the pattern of his eyelashes. People asked him questions and took his photograph. Later he saw his own image, taut and downcast, with a brooding look, on a poster that said *United Mining: Bringing Worlds Together*.

The effort of discovering his new orders placed him under constant strain. At first he was relieved to find he would not work as a guard, but after some time he almost wished for such orders: they would have been clear, at least, and he might have gone back to the Hold, and perhaps eased somebody's burden. Instead he went to the Doctors in the rooms. With Dr. Marjorie he made marks on a grid representing the Ships of the Fleet. He learned that his own Ship was not the only one: the Fleet drifted in space together, drawing sustenance from mines in enormous rocks. He wrote out numbers that symbolized distance and pressure. Dr. Marjorie, who had thick eyebrows, deep grooves in her cheeks, and a disgusted look, told him he was working at the level of a six-year-old child, and assigned him a tutor to help him catch up with the others. Thus far, his orders were clear, but he felt that something else was demanded of him, some insistent, increasingly urgent call radiated from Dr. Marjorie's deep-set eyes, and because he could not understand it and felt her growing frustration he was afraid of her, of the punishment she was surely preparing for him. What the punishment would be, and when it would fall, he did not know. He entered her room in a sickness of fear. Then one day, quite by accident, unaware of what he was doing, he pursed his lips in satisfaction over a problem he had solved, drumming his pencil on the table.

"You see!" cried Dr. Marjorie, startling him. "There is a harmony to it. A balance."

He saw that the secret command, which had eluded him so long, was to show his appreciation for Dr. Marjorie's subject, and through it, for Dr. Marjorie herself. Her eyes softened toward him, and he was no longer afraid.

The problem was that the unspoken orders were not always the same. Every room, every gathering, every scene came with its own specific demands, and even when he had learned the basic orders of a place there might be changes that stemmed from causes imperceptible to him. He watched the other students like him, whom he had learned to call *ankleted* instead of blueleg, and admired their shifting auras, how they could be angry and noisy with Dr. Gil, silent and grateful with Dr. Raymond, obedient and precise with Dr. Alvin, reacting easily to the rapid series of orders that made up their day, and emerging from it with enough energy for dancing. They took the boy to their dances. They taught him to drink the student liquor and lose his head. And it seemed to him that the volatility of their emotions, the sizzling whirl of the orders they obeyed, mirrored the fitful crackle of the blue anklets they wore in place of chains.

The Practice, he remembered, was the longing for understanding. It was a desire that began with an intake of breath. He breathed in knowledge with the humid air. He learned that many of his companions had family members who, through error or ill fortune, had been chained. Some of his friends asked him—drawing him aside, often at the end of the night, under the looming trees of the quad—if he had seen their kin. They were ashamed. Some of them wept. It was their greatest fear to be taken away in chains.

"Once you go down," they said, "you don't come up." The boy was the only person from the Hold they had ever met. They gave him gently mocking and awed nicknames: Miracle Kid, Luckman, Fluke. "Hey, Fluke," they asked him, "what do you want to be when you grow up? Driver, teacher, guard? Come on, look up! What's ahead?" It seemed to him that *up* was their favorite word. Their sensitivity to the countless flickering orders they received came from this overarching imperative: to stay upstairs, to stay free. They, and the elders, and the woman he called the professor, shared this fierce concentration, this drive for upward motion, an ardor that must extend, he thought, through all those who wore the anklet: the University janitors, office workers, and part-time teachers, and even the guards in the Hold, who all wore the anklet too. "Higher and higher," his new friends chanted at night, performing their intricate stamping steps that reminded him of chain dancing, jumping so that the legs of their trousers flared up for a moment and the snapping blue fire of anklets lit the dark.

Across the quad, the big rectangular windows of the Student Union shone in ordered rows, with silhouettes passing to and fro across them, the shapes of other students at a different dance, students who belonged to the same curious tribe as most of the University Doctors. The boy had been taught no name for this tribe. Instead of a name, they had names. They were Dr. Marjorie, Dr. Angela, Dr. Alvin, and Dr. Gil. The students were Ann and Pearl and Jack and others, on and on, always one at a time. What he knew about them was that they were far from the Hold. They talked to each other on phones, they took vacations on other Ships, and they stood entirely outside the dreadful intimacy that bound those in chains to those who wore the anklet, an intimacy of blood and resentment and fear of falling and tenderness and the strained, defiant determination to rise. He watched the silhouettes in the Student Union moving lightly, as if floating. None of these would ask him if he had seen their kin. He understood that they were individuals who could not be reduced to a group, but in his own mind, because they wore neither anklet nor chain, he called them Weightless.

When the boy had first come upstairs and learned to address his teachers as Doctor, he had thought they were all like the Doctor in the Hold: that their task was to loose his bolt in order to fit him with a larger one, suitable to his growth, with a longer chain. He had soon realized his mistake: *Doctor* was another name for teacher. But sometimes, when he learned something new, the feeling he had was not so different from what he had felt as a little boy, waking with a sore ankle and springing up to test the length of the chain. He remembered the day it was long enough for him to look out the door.

Now the door opened on a dripping world. On class trips, he visited orchards he had only imagined, until now, through the prophet's speeches: places of green sprouts and budding vines, where the chittering calls of birds and insects wafted from the trees. He saw creatures so huge he thought they must be Leviathan, but he learned they were cows. They gave him nervous, human glances from their lustrous eyes. Leaning over a bridge, he studied the shape of a river with the first professor he had met, the one he had once believed to be the blueleg witch.

He knew now that this woman was no witch. She was a teacher who helped him with his letters at night, sometimes bringing him a small bottle of Hold water. The professor was thin, with sharp, restless hands and a tired face. Her class was called Everyday Design. Propping her elbow on the bridge railing, she lectured the boy and the other students who clustered above the bright, curling water, explaining how her father, a water engineer, had cared for the continuity of life, and how the river worked toward this, both in its chemistry and in its beauty. She spoke of how the water caught the light, how people were drawn to its flash and froth, "a zone of freshness," she said, "of play." Couples strolled past; birds rose honking; a child knelt to launch a leaf boat. The boy began to think about the design of the Hold.

As they walked back to campus along the river, the students straying in groups, he drew near the professor and whispered, "Is that the River of Life?"

She looked surprised, then thoughtful. "Yes," she said. "All life comes from water."

The boy felt a tight excitement in his chest. So he had

found it! "This is the River that is a Sea?" he asked eagerly.

At that, the professor frowned. "Well, no," she said. "There is no longer any sea."

She told him that long ago, on old Earth, there had been a sea, and it had risen until it drowned the land. She called it a failure of design. The boy knew this story well, for he had heard from the prophet of the Flood that destroyed every living substance upon the face of the ground. His heart sank as he breathed the smell of the river that could not be a sea, for there was no sea. He would never find it, and he could never tell the prophet, for the prophet was lost to him, buried deep in the otherworld of the Hold, the starless country where the boy could never go.

As he thought of this that night, alone in his room, a tremor came over his body. This shaking had become a common thing. It came when he thought of the Hold, of the walls, of the chains, of how he had been prized out, sent hurtling toward the awful bourns of space, tossed up to the blueleg country where at night, through his window, he could see the greater window, the sky of the Ship, like a reservoir brimming with stars. He could see part of another Ship out there, its curve enveloped in cloudy light: one of the many Ships that made up the Fleet. He could see the shining of the rocks whose mines supported the Fleet and the sparkling flakes of the ferries moving to and fro. All of them together—the whole Fleet, and the rocks that hovered in the darkness with the tranquility of closed eyes—all of them, the boy had learned, were moving slowly in a majestic circle. They would tread this circle until the rocks were dry. And then the Fleet would move on until it discovered a new rich field of rocks. "For how long?" the boy had asked in his history class. "Forever," Dr. Raymond had said. Remembering this, the boy felt the trembling in his body grow stronger. Fighting it, gasping, he crawled underneath the bed.

There he slept, and dreamed of the drowned men. He saw again the wrecked room, the lengths of wire and pipe flung about in disarray. The floor knee-deep in water. He heard the voice of the prophet saying "Breathe, now," and he saw the drenched bodies in the light of the flare. The wall of a reservoir had burst where the gang of men was working, and the guards, to save themselves and the rooms beyond, had shut the door. Chained to each other and the wall, the men had whirled and risen and sunk and fought in the plunging dark until they died. The boy's gang had been ordered to clean the room afterward. He stood while the prophet instructed him to breathe among those whose breath had been stopped by a fist of water. The Doctor's boots splashed in the muck and he cursed in annoyance at the "waste" while he unlocked the bolts with the Mallet for the last time. And very still and holy the dead men looked when the boy and his gang had laid them out on the wagon with their souls exposed. Music rose around them, the gang singing a funeral chant as they wheeled the bodies to meet the compost train.

The boy awoke from the dream with his heart pounding. He thought of the river he had seen, its design, how it must touch the reservoirs below. No, it was not the River of Life. He felt the vibration of the dirge going through his bones, through every nail of the Ship.

> Cross my hands and cut my chain
> And carry me down to the compost train.

That day, in Dr. Alvin's class, he began to make a drawing of the drowned men, similar to the one he had once scratched on the wall of his cell, but worked out now in beautiful oily black pencil on a thick sheet of paper. He worked on it for many days, moving the pencil steadily, searching with it, breathing in time to the movement, inching gradually into a black and weblike dream from which he often had to be hauled, startled, by Dr. Alvin's voice. The boy would find himself back in the classroom, tingling and raked by light. And he would think: *I was there. That was the Practice.* He saw that his urge to draw was indeed the desire to breathe and know and live, and that this was why the prophet had sheltered his gift. But had the prophet known where it would lead him? The boy longed to lose himself in the branched and spiraling matrix of his drawing, to dig his way like a bulltick into the thickness of ghostly touch, but he feared it too: Was it like space, an abyss? Would he be lost there? He wished he could ask the prophet. He knew only that his night chills had decreased, that the drawing calmed him and helped him catch his breath. Dr. Alvin, moving through the room to check the students' progress, glanced at his picture and rumbled sardonically, "Interesting!"

Then one day Dr. Alvin announced a new classroom activity. It would be an exercise in figure drawing. Dr. Alvin, who had a big, impatient face fringed with beard, snapped his fingers at the door, and a guard came in. The guard was leading a young girl on a chain. She was naked. The boy automatically stood up and turned his back. No one else moved, though some of the other students glanced at the boy. He heard the familiar sound of the chain being locked to the wall.

"Hey." Dr. Alvin snapped his fingers.

The boy knew the sound was for him, but he did not move.

"Hey. Turn around there. Take your seat."

He stood, bound by something he could not name,

something he would not have thought to identify until that moment because it seemed to him a given, like being born with bones and flesh, a set of relations deeper than any order, a law that was subject to no conversion or alteration because it was lodged in the veins, in the blood, in the very fact of being a creature possessed of those attributes in a human shape. He stood by his desk and felt the air cold on his face and hands. He could hear Dr. Alvin shouting, but he could not turn around, and what chilled him was not the threat of punishment, which was something he understood, but the sudden confrontation with the absolute difference of the others around him, who sat in their chairs and looked at the girl. So then the code that bound him was not given. It was designed. It was a chain forged in the dark of the Hold, through the years of life in the depths, a chain whose glint he now recognized in the custom of turning away when members of a gang wished to be together at night, and in the delicate, labyrinthine rituals of the Meet Rooms.

Dr. Alvin was bellowing something about the great humanist tradition.

The boy realized that there was no chain on his leg. Just the dull blue buzz.

He turned, head down, opened his desk, pulled out his drawing of the drowned men, and rolled it up under his arm.

Then, his eyes still on the floor, he left the room.

~

After the meeting with the Dean, the meeting with the Provost, the emergency gathering of the scholarship committee, the appeal to the Board, and a rushed conversation with the jaded elder, who insisted on serving coffee, the woman went to the boy's room in the dormitory. She found him sitting on the bed among pencils and papers. His desk was empty and she put her own folders, notepads, and computer there. She plugged in the computer, jiggling its cord, which was mended with tape. "I thought we could do our homework together," she said.

"All right," said the boy.

He sat leaning back against the wall, staring at the angle of the ceiling. Outside the window, the evening lights reddened the quad. Faint voices streaked the air above the hum of fans.

The woman sat at the desk and turned the swivel chair toward the boy. "Or we could talk about what happened," she said quietly.

The boy shrugged. The woman remembered Alvin's heated face, yelling in the meeting about failed adjustment and disruptive behavior. Angela, trying to help, insisting that allowances had to be made for the boy, who was a victim of "cultural weakness." And Marjorie, who, when the woman began to speak, interrupted her, saying, "Remember how he hit you in the eye."

"But we don't have to talk about it," she said now.

The boy looked fixedly at the line of shadow where the ceiling met the wall. He swallowed.

The woman turned to the desk and opened her computer. Her throat felt dry. She thought of how close the boy had come to being expelled, how close they had all come to the end of the scholarship program. The appeal to the Board had saved it: Gil and Angela had defended the boy (it was best, they all agreed, that the woman remain silent, as her Hold connections might make her appear biased). Now she gazed at her screen, waiting for it to light up, thinking of her father, how he had described the life of ankleted people as a fragile shell. "It's thinner than a fingernail," he had said, "but a shell can last a long time, as long as there's a certain balance of pressure. Lose that"—he fluttered his fingers—"and everything is dust."

The woman's computer screen blinked. She rubbed her eyes. She was behind on her work; in a month she had to give a research talk to the personnel committee. She knew she should be much further along with her presentation by now. Her work with the scholarship committee had taken too much of her time, the boy had absorbed too much of her energy, she had spent too many evenings in this room, working with him, filling in the gaps left behind by his assigned reading tutor, complaining to Student Affairs about the reading tutor (a bored work-study student, untrained, surely the boy should have a professional tutor), going from Dean to Provost and back to beg for money to hire a new tutor, all the while teaching the boy herself. And there were the students she advised and the classes she taught (her evaluations had been poor last semester; students had called her disorganized), and the upcoming presentation. Everything was important: success was required in all areas. *The balance of pressure,* she thought. She opened the file called "Spaces of Play in Ankleted Communities."

> Unsupervised peer play among ankleted children is an understudied activity, and one with significant implications for environmental design theory. My current project foregrounds self-structured outdoor play among ankleted children aged three to twelve, located primarily in the Ninth and Twelfth Districts of Backhall . . .

She was pleased with most of this work, which analyzed the games played in the alleys and on the rooftops where she had grown up, the corners carved out by young children, the halls and palaces they could delineate with a twist of wire, and the forms made in the air by pieces of castoff or plastic sheeting. The problem was that in order to make her work legible to the personnel committee (legibility being an area where she must improve, she had been told), it was necessary to set up her argument with theories familiar to the discipline, to couch her work in terms her audience knew. The woman had been hired precisely in order to open new avenues of design research in the interest of Multiplicity (brought on through a special grant, on a different timeline from the regular hiring cycle, and so, her Department Chair had explained regretfully, she could not be issued a new computer, but must make do with a used one and line up with students to do her printing at the library). But in order to establish that this new research was in fact research, she must connect it with careful threads to the traditional archives, she must display a thorough grasp of established knowledge, and on pain of disgrace she must not mispronounce any venerable name.

Scrolling through her paper, she could see that it was not good enough. She tapped a key and waited for a connection to the library database. The screen dulled, then brightened. She already knew that the personnel committee would say her research lacked depth. And they would be right.

No depth, no advancement, no breakthrough. She thought of the off-ship conference she had missed again that year, held on one of the other Ships of the Fleet, one of those brilliant, mysterious vessels, filled with other schools and ideas, that twinkled softly in the evening sky. The woman had never been off-ship; in fact, none of the members of the Ring had ever traveled to a conference. Their proposals were always rejected. The jaded elder, who had given up writing proposals long ago, joked about what she called "the astonishing coincidence of our mediocrity." But the woman did not believe she was being rejected because of her anklet. She easily perceived the inadequacies in her work. She believed in knowledge, in thought, in the humanization of space, and in the refuge of the University, where one could still live for ideas. Still, she felt a painful twinge when she overheard her colleagues speaking of off-ship conferences, the weird cocktails that were served on the ferry, the shocking new theories proposed at celebrity panels, and the hilarious practical jokes at the hotel. Sitting at the boy's desk, she shook her head. She tapped the keys. *Envy degrades you,* she thought. Out of habit, her mind strayed to the low hiss of her anklet. It was a touchstone glimmering in the dark. Through it, she traced the presence of others. She sensed the boy sitting on the bed.

As if he had felt her thought reaching for him, he spoke. "The other students asked me, 'Don't you have Meet Rooms?'"

She turned to him in the chair. He was leaning forward now, cross-legged, elbows on his knees, studying the floor with a look of intent and anxious incomprehension, as if the tiles contained the chart of some unfathomable galaxy. "They said, 'Don't you have Meet Rooms in the Hold?' And I said yes. And everybody laughed. They asked, and I said yes, and they all laughed." He looked up at her, his face haggard, his jaw moving slightly.

Her heart flinched, touched in a sore place. "They don't understand," she told him. "They think they're called Meat Rooms. M-E-A-T. Not M-E-E-T. Two different words, same sound. Like we studied on the cards."

The boy looked at the floor again and she watched him absorb this message.

"I want to go back downstairs," he said.

She remembered her father seated in the evening, his face filled up with gentleness—or was it gentleness, could it have been something else? Suddenly she realized she didn't know what her father's face had held, and she was frightened. She thought of the Hold, its darkness, her childhood fears that her father would be taken away, arrested for some reason, that she would wake one morning to find him gone. She would not tell the boy how close he had come to being expelled downstairs. "I can't do that," she said.

He clasped his hands. He was shivering. Her own

hands felt light and unsteady on the arms of the chair. She had swallowed nothing all day but the jaded elder's coffee. "I'm going to get us some dinner," she said, and she walked down to the cafeteria and came back to the room with two covered trays. The boy took only the juice and the pudding, and she stopped herself from lecturing him about nutrition. He watched her eat her burger and vegetable sticks. Then he began to speak again, unfolding a careful argument which, she thought, he must have been composing in his head for hours, perhaps for days.

"When I was in the Hold," he told her, "I used to study something called the Practice." He spoke of a prophet who taught him about the River of Life. This was a River that was a Sea and the boy believed it was different from the river that ran through the center of the Ship. He told her that though he did not understand the nature of this River, he was bound to seek it no matter where it lay, and that all his efforts in drawing were a part of the calling to which the prophet had raised him, a Practice that began with the flow of breath. He told her he saw dead men in his dreams. He unrolled a paper on the floor, revealing a strange, complex, darkly rendered drawing: webs and nets with nodes that bulged like knucklebones. "I feel the dead," he said. "I don't understand it. I have to see the prophet."

The woman took a breath. She prepared to begin her

argument about opportunity. But she found she could not begin while looking at his face, the lines of it gaunt and still and sad against the lines of his drawing. She remembered, suddenly, a party when she was a child: her parents had invited several people to their apartment, all ankleted, with ordinary jobs for their caste, as she learned when her father introduced them—nurse's assistants, drivers, cooks—but they were unlike anyone she had met before. They sat close together, their hands resting on their knees. A deep, heavy feeling came into the room. The anklet dimmed on her small leg. No one noticed the paper plates she had decorated with crayons. She cried, and her mother took her away, whispering that the visitors were her father's old school friends: people from the Hold.

Now, looking at the boy, she sank again in the weight of that long-ago evening, its dismal, colorless air, as if no time had passed, as if time would never pass, as if change itself changed nothing. She felt she was suffocating; she realized she was holding her breath. She let it out. Then something occurred to her, and she said, "Wait."

She turned to the computer. "Wait a second," she said, linking into the University files. She had remembered an old project proposal, written up years ago by the jaded elder, one of many such projects rejected by the Board.

"I have an idea," she said. "It might not work. It's just

an idea." She clicked rapidly through the files. There it was: "Community Engagement Proposal." She opened the file. *I should have eaten dinner hours ago,* she thought, as a rush of well-being coursed up her spine.

"Okay," she said. "This is it. I'm not promising anything."

The boy had come to stand behind her. "What is it?"

"A way of getting downstairs. Not to stay. But to see your prophet. *Maybe.*" She clicked, copying the file. "I'm going to work on this. And I want you to do your homework."

I don't have time for this, she thought, with a sparkling surge of recklessness. *My research is sitting there! And now I'll be up all night!* But she felt that connecting the boy to the Hold was the only way to keep him upstairs, to keep from losing him, and the scholarship program, for good. And she felt something else: a force moving through her like a trail of light, warming, expanding, extending. For the first time that day, she felt alive.

The boy returned to the bed. For a time she forgot about him, and everything else, immersed in work.

Then he said softly, almost whispering, "I feel it."

She turned her chair. He raised his eyes from his anklet in fear and wonder, the light of it blue on his skin, glittering wanly but steadily against the bedsheet, its tinny radiance touching his papers, the dinner tray, the meal he had mangled halfheartedly, and even, she thought, the surface of his eyes, the ghost of a shimmer playing over his dark, fascinated, and awestruck gaze.

"Like you told me," he breathed. "In the buzz. I can feel it. I feel you in the room."

2

The Horizon

GOING DOWNSTAIRS HE COULD FEEL the professor's fear in the tick of her anklet soft yet sharp like the needle-feet of an insect creeping over his skin, he could feel the meditative, vaguely curious and amused presence of the guard at their side in the lift, he could feel the guards downstairs in the Hold, feel them going about their tasks, exactly as the professor had said: as if they were strung together, a chain of lights. This chain extended far, upstairs and down. The distant lights grew fainter. He tried to count them, reaching as far as the feeling could extend, this sensation he had been testing for three weeks now, since he had first felt it in his room with the professor: the slender, volatile presence of others.

"Wake up, son," said the guard in the lift. "We're here."

The door opened onto the long bare passage. He had forgotten how dark it was. His skin, sunk in dampness so long, prickled in the keen dry air.

He gave the guard the number of his gang. As they

walked down the sloping corridor, the boy's eyes adjusted to the sickly beams of the little nubs high on the walls, the drear and constant half-light of the Hold, so different from the shifting light upstairs, with its brilliance and variety of color. He breathed the familiar smell. He heard a clang somewhere in the network of tunnels. A cry. The professor shuddered. He could feel her throbbing heart. He wondered if it was possible for the feeling to go the other way: Could he send her a message, as well as receive it? He tried to send her calm.

A failure. Her heart jumped. She stopped and grabbed his arm. "What was that?"

"I don't know," he said, frightened by her reaction.

Her nails dug into his arm. "What was that what was that?" she repeated, her eyes huge and scared in the dimness.

"Easy, sis," said the guard. "You want me to get you a chair?"

"No," the professor whispered. "I'm all right."

"Now, see," said the guard, "this is why I don't like this kind of scheme. With all due respect. I don't know why you want to come down here, sis. A nice lady like you."

"I'm fine," the professor said.

They followed the guard up a ladder to the work level, where the prophet was scraping slop. The boy's eyes swam with tears at the sight of his former gang, the gleam of the little old shanks of the prophet tensing as he worked, the crude bulk of the chain connecting mate to mate. The men looked at the boy from the corners of their eyes. It was the well-known, tiny, piercing greeting of the Hold. The boy gave a sob. He knew he was coming back to them as a blueleg boy. He knelt by the prophet and pressed his brow to the floor, to the still-warm slop that had spattered there.

"Hey!" said the guard, coming to haul him up by the waist.

The boy gave in at once to the touch of the guard. *Design,* he thought in a daze.

But the guard did not beat him. He took the boy's chin and gave it a gentle shake. "Hey. Look at me. Are you there? All right. You're all right, son. You just fainted. Is this the one you want? The old fellow? Okay. Let's get him and get out of here."

The guard unlocked the prophet's chain from the others, talking all the while, repeating to the professor that he didn't agree with this scheme, that with all due respect it was never a good idea for people upstairs, nice people like the professor and the boy, to get involved in down-stairs business. Casually, brusquely, he yanked the prophet into the halfway room and hosed him down, and kindly and carefully he wiped the boy with a cloth, telling him not to worry, anybody could faint on their first time down, he himself had lost his entire appetite when he first started work.

"You'll be a man of iron one day," he said. The boy felt the guard's anklet glinting affably. "Man of iron. Tell you what. You want to hold him?"

"Yes," said the boy. He took the prophet's chain and wrapped it about his wrist, pulling it tight enough to mark the skin. He gazed into the prophet's depthless, shining eyes. He could feel the prophet as he felt the professor and the guard through the anklets, but with less effort. He felt so much, the disinfectant particles on the prophet's skin, on his own skin, he felt the traces of slop, the troughs where the slop came falling down, where the men scraped up what splashed on the floor, and above he felt the network of pipes, the barns where animals groaned, the feed, the light. *So we are below the cows,* he thought. His awareness expanded, then shrank again, becoming concentrated on the bright face of the prophet, the secret, watchful, waiting stillness of the face he loved.

"Look at the kid," the guard chuckled. "He's a natural."

They went down to the boy's old cell, where the guard took the prophet's chain and locked it to the wall, apologizing because there was no furniture, no decent place for the boy and the professor to sit. He went away and came back with two metal stools. The boy and the prophet had already sat down by the wall. The professor, standing, was looking at the boy's pictures. The boy got up and sat on a stool and the guard explained to the professor that he would be just outside, directly outside the door in case anything happened. On his way out he knocked his boot carelessly into a small pyramid of castoff objects, somebody's collection. The pieces rolled on the floor.

He left the door halfway open, but the boy couldn't see him so he got down off the stool and touched his brow to the floor and sat up again on his knees, weeping quietly in the manner of the Hold. "I didn't mean to be made blueleg," he whispered. "They did it to me."

The prophet said he knew. He embraced the boy and made space for him on the small gray blanket whose rough, brittle-feeling surface sent shivers through the boy's hand, shivers through his leg where it touched his skin, full of old nights, all the nights of his life. He felt the professor standing behind him, he felt her move, and he turned just in time so that he and the prophet, looking at the professor, said in unison "Watch the jakes!" as she was about to slip in.

The professor started back from the edge of the hole where freezeflies gamboled.

The boy and the prophet looked at each other, both on the verge of laughter. The boy wiped his tears on his sleeve. As the professor came to sit shakily on a stool, rubbing her elbows in the cold, the boy explained why they had come. He told the prophet about his dreams and his pictures and how he entered the web of the dead and felt the drowned men close about him, as though he were floating, as though he were chained and floating with them in water. He said they went on and on, the dead, much farther than the twelve drowned bodies he'd seen while waking. He said he did not know how far they went, and he was afraid.

The prophet took his hand. He spoke to the boy with the fluid sounds of the Hold, and the boy realized how much he had missed this smooth polishing of syllables, and how tight he had held his own jaw upstairs, mimicking the clipped speech of guards. The prophet said he too had known the web the boy had touched. He believed it was the Practice itself made plain to the inner sense. But whether it was the web of the dead or the living or both together he could not say. "Sometimes," he said, "I see my child."

The old man paused and looked up at the professor on the stool. "I had a little child," he explained, "and she was taken off."

"Taken off?" said the professor.

"To another Ship," said the boy. He pointed to the wall, where he had drawn the child.

"That's not—I don't think that's possible," the professor said. "Not off-ship. The ferries are restricted."

The prophet was quiet, his chin with its tuft of beard sunk on his chest. Then he raised his head and told the boy to look at his picture. "Look," he said, "how you took what was there and made it something else. You took that line, that some other person drew, and you made it into a Ship. Who made that line? Somebody dead. We don't know. But you made this picture together, you worked on this picture together, you and the dead." His voice gathered strength and vibrancy. "How did you know what to do? How did the dead know what you wanted? It had to be the Practice. Something linked you together, like the kneebone to the thighbone. And you knew it, felt it. Like a game of Scatter."

The boy's anklet twitched. He felt the professor sit up on her stool. Her sudden attention. "Scatter?" she said.

The prophet looked up at her. He talked in his rusty, throbbing voice and the professor leaned down to listen, straining to catch the words. The boy could feel her effort and he could feel the aged weariness of the prophet, who was worn out and soon to die. He remembered how the prophet used to say, "Death is on my shoulder." And the boy would say, "No, no." But now he felt it. *Cross my hands and cut my chain.*

And welling up through the age and exhaustion and torment the boy felt something else, insistent, faltering, aglow. *His breath,* he thought.

~

The woman came up from the Hold with a gasp, blinking in the light. The air of the security station tasted so sweet, she thought she was outdoors. And when she did step outdoors, out of the station into a rosy afternoon glistening with the freshness of watered trees, she almost wept from the kindness of it, the balmy, sheltering breeze of the fans. She realized she was clinging to the boy's arm; she quickly let go.

"All right, professor?" he said.

He regarded her calmly, his small frame upright and untroubled, more comfortable, she thought, than he had been before the trip down. Leaf shadows played on his face but he seemed beyond them, out of reach and glad to be so, in touch with elsewhere, with the dark.

She nodded. She walked with him to his dorm and he waved her a cheerful goodbye from the steps, fulfilled, she thought, as if he had drunk deeply of the water her father had loved, immersed himself in a necessary spring, while she was crumbling, stunned, undone by the same experience, hurrying back to her apartment, hiding her tears from passersby, bumping into poles and fences. In her kitchen she stripped and stuffed her clothes in the garbage, flinging her hair clip after them.

She got in the shower and scrubbed herself hard with

the brush. The people down there, so many. The cold. The prophet who lost his child. She sat down in the shower. Then she stood up again. She had to go, she had to dress, to be at Gil's house for dinner, to tell him about the first day of the project. The words *community engagement project* clacked inside her head. She remembered Gil's zeal as he helped her present the proposal to the Board. Angela and Marjorie had signed it too, but the jaded elder had refused, even though she was the original author of the project. "Already tried it," she said. "But we have support now," the woman had countered. "Gil, Angela—lots of people." The jaded elder had chuckled low in her throat. "Then you don't need me," she said. "It's mining people that get things done in the Age of Mines." And although she had given her blessing to the woman's efforts, she would not get involved in the community engagement project. She would not join another committee, she said; and, laughing, she had called herself "a worn-out tire."

In the shower, the woman remembered that laugh. She recalled the voice of the prophet. His words reverberated around her, slurred and breaking like falling water, telling of the child who was taken away, of the River that was a Sea, of the open graves in the Valley of Dry Bones. Once, he said, on ancient Earth, there was a Horizon, and to gaze on it was to look neither up nor down. *Look out,* he said, pointing a finger. He put his hands to his ribs. He said the breath expanded the body in all directions.

Kneebone thighbone hipbone. She turned the shower off. She got out, went to the garbage, and took out the clothes she had worn in the Hold. She put the clothes in the laundry hamper. She rooted in the trash for her hair clip, found it, washed it, dried her hands, and got dressed.

Passing her desk, she paused and looked down at the draft of her research paper. The words of the first paragraph stood out strangely. It was as if she were perceiving them through a telescope, as if she'd written them in a different life, and at the same time the letters seemed brighter than before. Deep blue.

> Unsupervised peer play among ankleted children is an understudied activity, and one with significant implications for environmental design theory. My current project foregrounds self-structured outdoor play among ankleted children aged three to twelve, located primarily in the Ninth and Twelfth Districts of Backhall, as a form of critical social and spatial sense-making. Games such as Pick and Scatter, categorized by my informants as "nowhere games"—a term to which I shall return— share several characteristics of interest to the theorization of informal design and the study of everyday life, most importantly (1) a slender materiality (the games

require only a small amount of castoff to play, in some cases a single hairpin or nail), and (2) a correspondingly vast symbolic field, which, as I will show, increases in proportion to the paucity and inferiority of physical objects . . .

She went outside, into the clement light. There was still time before she had to be at Gil's house. She walked across campus, following the river, past the Commissary where a video poster beamed *United Mining: Eternal Springtime,* then through the park and the busy café district. She entered an ankleted neighborhood where the blocks rose without variation, the streets uneven and devoid of green. Some children were playing Scatter with a broken cup. She sat on a stoop and watched them, thinking *breath* thinking *Practice* thinking *like a game of Scatter* thinking *Bones.* "When you play Scatter," the prophet had said, "when it's really good, it's because you all move as one, as if one knows where the ball will fall before the other kicks it. And how does that one know? It's because they've played together, felt and thought of each other in movement and stillness. It's the Practice." This he had said in the gloom, in the near-freezing stench of the Hold. The meager bulb above him shedding a single ray on the curve of his brow. Sitting on the stoop, the woman could see, above the rim of the darkening sky, a distant Ship winking. "Outside!" a child yelled. The woman put her head down on her knees.

She sat there too long. The streetlamps were lit when she arrived in Gil's neighborhood and she could see into the houses, the windows flushed with molten radiance. Children were riding bicycles in the street. Voices called them. A rich, invigorating scent rose from the sprinkled gardens. She crossed Gil's backyard, stepping over stray flowerpots and tools, and entered the kitchen. Gil's wife, Rachel, was drying her hands on a towel and she hugged the woman and told her it was no problem she was late. "Let me get you a glass of wine," she said.

The woman had been to Gil's house many times. His two children called her Auntie. After dinner, Rachel clapped her hands and said, "Bed!"—the signal for the children to run away squealing while Rachel chased them until their voices faded in the back rooms of the house.

Gil shook his head in mock disgust. "Savages!" he said. He refilled the woman's wineglass and then his own, and leaned to switch on the outdoor lights, which sequined the air outside the big picture window with a simulation of fireflies.

He wanted to hear all about the community engagement project. The woman told him, at first with a vague reluctance that surprised her, then with increasing enthusiasm, fired as usual by Gil's energy, at this table where they had made so many plans. Here they had devised the Departmental Renaming Initiative and the University Scholarship for the Chained. Jokingly, Gil called it their campaign table. Now he shoved the dirty dishes aside to make room for his computer.

"Right," he said. "So we're looking at something mystical. A sort of belief system."

"Maybe," said the woman. "I'm not sure yet what it is."

"Uh-huh, uh-huh," said Gil, typing. He ran his hand through his hair so it stood on end—a typical gesture when he was thinking—and read over what he had written. "That's good. Exploring new forms of belief. Angela will love it. Do you think we could call it a kind of religion?"

The woman said she didn't know. The term seemed strange. She talked about the child who was taken away, and Gil said maybe it was an aesthetic practice she was targeting, a fantastical mode of storytelling. He deleted "New Forms of Belief" in favor of "New Forms of Narrative." The woman watched him type. Every so often he shook back the big bracelet on his wrist. She remembered the prophet saying how the Practice outlasted failure, how it failed and failed and continued to exist. "Here it is," the old man had said. "Right here. In this room." He cupped his hands, in which a flake of light from the bulb above him nestled as if alive. She remembered the words he had used, their antique flavor, how they seemed like castoff carried in the mouth, over the years.

"I think it's a strategy," she said.

Gil paused. "Yeah. That's good. A narrative strategy."

"A *survival* strategy," the woman said excitedly. "I think it's something like castoff. You know, the research I'm doing right now, it's all about castoff, about making things out of broken, discarded stuff. What if this is the same kind of thing? This Practice. But the materials are so frail they're almost intangible."

"Whoa," laughed Gil. "Slow down."

But heated by wine and still shaken by her recent trip to the Hold the woman could not slow down. The firefly lights in the window flashed like colliding thoughts. "It's what we do, don't you see?" she cried. "It's how we live—by collecting the castoff of the universe. We miners, we're scavengers. Why not learn survival strategies from those who have survived?"

Gil took a sip of wine. He said it was really great, really stimulating, what she was saying, they just had to word it right, to be careful how they expressed it, to emphasize the difference of the chained, according to the principle of Multiplicity. "We don't want to look like we're using their ideas," he cautioned. "Stealing them. You know?"

The woman's heart shrank. "Of course," she said, flustered. "I didn't mean—"

"Oh, I know," said Gil, filling her glass. "I know you meant it in the most respectful way. I think using a word like narrative will make that clear. Or maybe folklore. What do you think? A New Study of the Folklore of the Chained."

She nodded. Gil pushed back his hair and went on typing briskly. He had a gift for persuasion. After the boy's disastrous run-in with Alvin, Gil had argued eloquently to the Board that exposure to different cultures and worldviews was a key part of education. While it was true that Alvin had lost class time through the boy's disruption, said Gil, the students had gained something of lasting value. The regular students, the ones with phones, had received a lesson in difference. It was *good* for them, said Gil. And the boy had not been expelled.

Everything is good for them, the woman thought suddenly. The thought startled her. Its violence.

Gil's bracelet clicked against his keyboard. The woman remembered a line from the jaded elder's draft of the project, now deleted: *Can the University be a place of both training and transformation?*

~

It is not the boy. It is not the woman. It is not the prophet. It is not the child. It is the mesh. Entanglement. Vibration, bright-

ness, scent. It is what binds. It is the knowledge that does not divide itself. It is the voice of the prophet saying once on ancient Earth, there was a Horizon, saying don't look up and don't look down, look out, his voice produced by breath and pressure and rhythmic beating of vocal cords, a resonance caught and quivering in the ears of the boy and the woman. It is resonance. It is an echo in the bowels of the Ship. It is what wakes. It knocks the wall. It sets the nervous system trembling. The heart melts and runs, the joints of the loins are loosed, the knees smite together. It awakens to itself.

It awakens. Its desire is to communicate with itself. It is at home in all things, it does not know exile. The hand grips the charcoal. It is crystal. It is structure. It is base. It is electric, ductile, waxy, aromatic. The carbon grips the carbon. Forms arise. The children run. The cattle drink at the river. The prophet dreams. A thought strikes the woman. An image haunts the boy. The child opens her eyes, her lashes curled. It is tendrillar, lustrous, brittle, soft, viscous, stinging, earthy. It is the tie that binds. It is design. The hand grips. The drowned return. It is the bond, the chain that grows in all directions: for the Chain of Being is not up and down. It is the child. It is the prophet. It is the woman. It is the boy.

~

In the afternoons now the boy and his professor went

down to the Hold to sit with the prophet. Sometimes they listened to him and sometimes the three of them spoke together, words glancing to and fro in the grainy darkness of the cell where the boy hunched close to the prophet on the frayed old blanket. The boy would hold the prophet's chain, his fingers curled in the links. The rugged metal slowly warmed beneath his hand. He told the prophet of everything he had seen: the river, the herds of cattle, the orchards filled with pleasant fruits, the stars. All of those things were real, they weren't just stories. The prophet's eyes glowed. "I knew they were real," he said. "I just didn't know they were so close." He said he could feel his awareness growing now with every breath and his stories were changing, taking in the levels and contours of the Ship.

The boy gathered pieces of castoff from the floor and used them to map the Ships of the Fleet and the sere untenanted rocks from which they took their life, and the professor, who no longer sat on a stool but crouched with the boy and the prophet on the floor, reached out to adjust and correct his diagram. Her anklet, like the boy's, made a little blue pool in the dark. She picked up a piece of wire someone had twined into a circle. She asked the prophet about castoff, about the little heaps of stuff lying here and there in the cell, about collections and games. The boy could feel her interest crackling. She liked anything she could learn about toys and rhymes, the things people made and said for themselves. The prophet laughed and hummed old songs and sometimes the three of them played a game of Pick, tossing castoff, building imagined castles in the gloom. The professor said this was the only way a new shape could enter the world. This was design, which created nothing, but rearranged the things that were. Each shape, she said, was a new way of being. And the prophet told her that this was what he called the Practice. "Wheels within wheels," he said.

Sometimes the talk of the prophet and the professor went beyond the boy, so that he felt like a little child grasping the winking threads of adult speech, but sometimes he felt very old, as if his two teachers were the children and he was watching them from a remoteness of cold night. He saw them rolling their toys on the floor. He heard them speak of newness. But he could see no space for anything new in the Fleet's grim architecture, its repetitive cells and chambers, its iced spokes suspended in the void, the inexorable sameness of its lines. Sometimes when they met the prophet was sick and lay on his side and the boy stroked the old man's back until he slept, thinking that all over the Fleet old people lay on their sides like this, breathing their last breaths into the murk. The professor had tried to bring the prophet some blankets and a suit of clothes, but this was against regulations. "You'd start a riot!" the guard exclaimed. "Let one of them get some extra cloth, they'll tear each other apart." While he spoke, the boy bowed his head until it touched the prophet's shoulder. And the prophet, lying on his side, breathing shallowly in the cold, spoke to the boy in his high, cracked little voice. "You're all right," he said. "You'll be all right. Just start with one. One breath." And the boy clung to the old man as if drowning.

At the end of the month, Dr. Angela invited the boy to speak about the community engagement project on Multiplicity Day. Dr. Angela had taut pinprick eyes, a long, sleek braid of hair, and a dog named Baby she walked on a plastic chain. "Hey!" she said, meeting the boy as he was crossing the quad. He stood awkwardly, not daring to move as the dog snuffled at his feet. Dr. Angela said not to worry about Baby. "He won't hurt you." She understood, she said, that the boy was not used to large animals. She knew how strange everything must be to him: the air, the light, meeting people with different ideas, learning to eat new foods.

"I bet you miss that pap," she said, twinkling.

The boy nodded. With his ability to read the orders of the Weightless, honed for several months now, he understood that Dr. Angela's particular demand was for an easy camaraderie and warmth. She liked him to agree with her, to laugh, and to shake his head incredulously, as if astonished by how much she knew about him, so he obeyed while she told him things about himself. He thought of it as feeding her. And her face swelled and brightened, as if she were actually eating.

"Listen," she said, "I'm organizing some events for Multiplicity Day. It's tomorrow. Have you heard about it? You're probably already involved."

"No," said the boy.

"What?" Dr. Angela cried. "You're not? I can't believe that!" She took out her phone and began to tap. "I'm making a note to myself. We need to find out how this happened. I am *so* sorry. You're exactly the kind of person who should be highlighted!"

She apologized for a long time. The boy was late to Dr. Raymond's class, and Dr. Raymond said, "Look who decided to join us." He bowed deeply to the boy. "Welcome, O King." The class snickered. They had been learning about the principles of democracy.

The next day the boy found himself seated on the stage in the auditorium, a harsh light concentrated on his forehead. Dr. Angela introduced him to a crowd of Weightless faces, with a few of his ankleted friends waving from the back. He looked at his friends, and, reaching out tentatively through his anklet, just enough to sense them, but not to frighten them as he had done with the professor, he felt their sympathy, their hectic energy, and their contempt for what they secretly called Imbecility Day. He drew on these feelings, as once, in the Hold, when he was sick or tired, he had allowed the other men in his gang to pull him along with the chain. He wished the professor was there, but she was giving her own presentation to the Doctors. "It's too bad she can't come," Dr. Angela had agreed. "But the program's so busy! And, anyway, I'll be there."

Dr. Angela asked him questions. He heard his own voice amplified by the microphone. Disjointed words. He tried to go back and fix them. His mouth felt parched. "Tell us about your prophet," she said, and although it was a clear and direct order, he found it difficult to obey. The prophet, he said, was old, and still alive. The light burned. He heard his disembodied voice talking out of the air. Dr. Angela explained to the audience that the prophet was not really old, that age worked differently among the chained. So the old were not old and his voice was not his voice and the room, he felt suddenly, was not real, he felt himself slipping, he tried to tie himself to his body, to ground himself in the grating edge of sound as he cleared his throat, in the sweat at his hairline, in his anklet above all, that tenuous link, and he felt the professor in another room, she was making a speech and she was afraid. She feared the Doctors. Their judgment. He saw her upraised head. *I can almost hear her voice,* he thought, startled, and then he did hear it. *Everyday life,* she said. Stunned and blinking, he struggled back into his body, back to the room where he was, where the Weightless students lounged in their seats, whispered together, and entered notes in their phones to receive their extra credit.

He wanted to ask the professor, or at least the other ankleted students, what this meant, if they'd ever tried to push energy out through their anklets, if they'd ever seen someone, heard someone, through the blue buzz. But it was Multiplicity Day, and so he was never alone with the members of the Ring. He saw the professor at the Multiplicity and Togetherness Banquet, wearing the same high collar that had appeared to him in his mind. Her face looked strained, but she smiled when she saw him. She asked him about his talk, and he said it was all right. "How was yours?" he asked. "Fine." Around them, the Weightless drank punch.

He returned to his room, feeling a hazy fringe of un-reality all about him. In the night, he awoke suddenly from a sound sleep. He still slept under the bed, and now he crawled out and sat up on his knees and looked out the window where a nearby Ship hung glittering in the dark. He could only see part of its curve. The whole Ship was round, the professor had taught him, like a wheel. His own Ship was the same: a Wheel in the Middle of the Air. The Hold was in the center. Somewhere, perhaps on that Ship, perhaps on another, in some other Hold, the prophet's child was sleeping or trying to sleep. He reached for the papers strewn on the floor and felt for a stub of pencil and began to draw with only the stars and the foreign Ship for light. *Once on ancient Earth, there was a Horizon.* What could it mean, to look neither up nor down? *Look out.* The Horizon must be everywhere, in all directions.

Hunched and alert, wrinkling the paper with the force of his movements, he drew the prophet, he breathed himself into the prophet reaching for his child. And the child was gone, torn out. And the prophet reached. The boy remembered his own mother. He remembered how, when he was small, when he was taken from her, the older boys and men in his gang had comforted him, telling him he would see her on the feast day. Every day he asked if it was the feast day, and when the day came at last, when they entered the freezing hangar veiled with the clammy, threadbare mist of their breath, one of the men scooped the boy up and lifted him on his shoulder so that he could see over the welter of the crowd. Everywhere people were holding up children and calling. He saw his mother, far away. Her face like a fingertip. Her hand. He cried and cried. He was crying now in his room in the dormitory, crushing and tearing the paper, tears making his picture a black and smeary mess. He felt the wetness of his tears breaking up the marks of his pencil, eating the paper, he felt the grit of the pencil dissolving into his skin, grit from where, from the rocks they were mining outside, from the dead on the compost train, from old Earth, from the stars that were long before old Earth. He felt the Ship around him humming with life. He felt the drowned, their bodies inside the Ship, the dirt, the orchards, his body, his aching skin. He drew with his hands, his tears. He felt the prophet's heart twanging like a plucked wire. To have a child and to lose that child. The child's body. Not to know what had happened, where she was. Not to be able to save her, protect that body. He felt it like a fire in his brain.

It was a fire that would never end. He traced it, followed it, let it take him. He remembered the day they told him his mother had died. He remembered the drowned men. He felt himself entering the enormous web that stretched away from the Ship in all directions. If the Horizon was everywhere, then there was no wrong place to begin. *Start with one,* he thought. He would start with the living. He would begin with the child. And as if in response to his resolution, the great web tensed and quivered and he knew. He knew exactly where she was.

~

The woman's anklet jerked an instant before she heard the knock on the door. She sat up in bed, disoriented. The clock read *04:12*. The jolt at her ankle, the impact, set her heart thudding. She had felt something like it only once before: on the day she had first gone down to the Hold with the boy.

She wanted to think, to understand the significance of this, but he was pounding at the door. She threw on her robe and went to open it. The boy stood in the cool, damp night beneath the security lamp, his face clear and ardent and suffused with elation.

"I found her," he said. "I found the prophet's child."

She could feel the delirium bubbling from him through his anklet, as if he were drunk.

"Have you been to a party?" she asked.

He laughed. "No, professor. The party is starting right now. Come on. We have to get downstairs before they see us."

He wouldn't come inside, wouldn't accept her offer of breakfast, and at last, when he threatened to leave without her, the woman agreed to get dressed. For an instant, as she glanced at herself in the mirror, she thought that what she was doing was risky, that she should fetch Gil instead. If the boy was having some kind of crisis, they needed to get him to the University Hospital as quickly as possible, with a minimum of fuss. But she recoiled from the thought of contacting Gil, of exposing the boy in this state. If she could just get him to calm down, go back to his room, maybe it would pass and no one would know.

But there was no calming him down. He slid down the railing of the steps outside her apartment, laughing, moisture spraying from his clothes. He ran through the open gate, came back to tug her arm, dashed off again. She hurried to catch up, following him through the quad, the sports field, the deep weeds by the river. The glow of day was blue in the air, her trousers were drenched to the knee, and the boy moved lightly, laughingly over the bridge, with a marvelous confidence, a sense of purpose that frightened her as they entered the industrial district, where towers loomed through the fog that billowed about the wall of the Ship. The boy did not seem to be lost. If anything, his sense of direction seemed stronger here, his eyes more brilliant and determined than ever. She felt cold. The district was waking up. Vehicles moved, beeping quietly. Lights swept between the buildings.

"In here," said the boy. He pulled her into a dark building with a chemical stink and made her crouch with him behind a row of barrels.

"Okay," she whispered. "Maybe now it's time to—"

"Shh!"

She waited. Casting her mind toward her anklet, she scanned the building and felt a pair of workers approach their hiding place. She knew the boy had noticed them first. There was something strange about it: his sensitivity. She held her breath. If the workers weren't fully aware of their surroundings, if they didn't decide to scan the area, didn't think of their anklets, they wouldn't realize the boy and the woman were there.

The workers drew near. "And I said, 'If you don't want to live here, fine. But you signed the lease.'"

"Uh-huh."

"And she said, 'I want to sublet my half.' 'Your half of what?' I said."

They passed by. Cautiously, tremblingly, the woman released her breath. "Okay," she whispered. "Okay. That's good. Now we have to go."

The boy nodded. "Come on."

But he didn't leave the building. He flitted around the barrels and knelt beside a large bolt in the floor. There was a wheel attached to the bolt and the boy turned it until he could open the lid of a vertical tunnel that led down under the building. Grunting, he lifted the lid and shoved it so that it fell back on the floor with a bang that made the woman start and scan the area nervously. No one was coming, but this, she realized, looking at the boy, might be cause for worry rather than relief.

He swung his legs into the hole. "There's a ladder," he said.

"Wait," said the woman. "You can't go down there."

"I told you," he said. "I've found the prophet's child. We go down here and through some hallways and wait for the ferry. It's going to the other Ship. And we go to their Hold, and we'll find her. She's splitting rocks right now."

"Wait," she said again. "You don't know that. There's no way you could know that. Listen. You can't go downstairs that way. You can't just get on a ferry. You have to have clearance." She struggled to keep her tone light; her heart was racing. "You're not authorized to go down that ladder. If you do, your anklet will set off an alert. It's dangerous. Please."

He looked up at her in the ashen air of the building, sitting with his legs in the hole, skinny, gawky, with something disordered in his appearance: a fuzzy, feral, half-grown look.

"I want to help you," she said.

"I know." His hands had tightened on the edge of the hole. "But you're not going to."

"I am," she said. "Don't worry. You're not in any trouble. I'm just going to get Dr. Gil, okay?"

"Professor. Don't do that, professor. I can see her splitting rocks. She's using that one hand because the other one has a pain. She wears a tiny mask. I found her, don't you see? I picked her out. I made this shape. And now it's making me."

He was raving. The woman scanned for the nearest worker. The two who had passed them were not far away, and she ran to them and begged them to get help. She gave them Gil's name. One of them went to the office to ask their superior to make a call, while the other, a small, wiry person with a patient face, accompanied the woman back to where the boy sat. The boy was weeping unrestrainedly. "My stars," the worker said. "My blazing, ever-loving stars. Hold on, son. It's too early in the day." The woman began to cry and the worker said, "Don't *you* start. Come on, sis. Here. Sit down on this crate."

After an agonizingly long time, Gil arrived. His hair stood up and his face looked gray and waxy.

"Oh, Gil," said the woman. "Thank you."

"Leave us," Gil told the worker.

"Right away," the worker said, and went out.

"I'm so sorry," said the woman, standing and wiping her eyes with her palms. "I didn't know what to do. He just—it was four A.M. Four A.M., I think. He woke me up. He was like this. I tried to calm him down, but he just kept running. I didn't know what—"

"Stand up," Gil told the boy.

His voice chilled the woman. The boy had stopped

crying, but he did not move. He looked at the woman with terrible silence, comprehension, and despair.

"Stand up out of that hole," said Gil.

The boy took a shuddering breath.

"Maybe your cousin," the woman whispered. "Your cousin, the Doctor ..."

Gil took his phone from his pocket. She thought he was going to call the Doctor, but instead he pointed the phone at the boy and said: "Up. Out of that hole." He held the phone straight at the boy, pressing it with his thumb, and the boy's leg with the anklet flew up and planted itself on the floor. The boy scrabbled at the floor with his hands and struggled to his feet at the edge of the hole. His foot with the anklet took a firm step forward. And as he righted himself, standing now, his arms flung out for balance, the woman realized he was in lockstep.

He came toward Gil with the dreadful, lunging, uncouth lockstep motion, the ankleted foot stamping inexorably forward, the rest of the body catching up. He was beside the woman before she found her voice. "Please," she said, her lips numb. "I'm sure that's not necessary. He'll be glad to come with us now."

Gil looked at her coldly. "I have a class at eight o'clock," he said. "It is unbelievable, *unbelievable* what you've done. Dragging me out here!"

His thumb twitched on the phone and as the woman

apologized she felt the clamp. She felt it close on her ankle. *Snap.* She was in lockstep. Her leg and the boy's leg shot forward exactly at the same instant and stamped on the floor. She reeled, arms whirling, like a clown in a comedy show.

"Gil!" she cried. "Don't!"

Gil was behind them, holding the phone. The boy and the woman marched in rhythm out the door and into the street. Gil was talking but she couldn't understand him. She had to walk, sobbing, jerking awkwardly, cringing from the pain as her leg plunged forward, striving to minimize the jarring thump of each step, to arrange her body around it, realizing that resistance, or even a mistake, any failure to comply, could cause a sprain or even a break. *Fragility,* she thought. Her ears were ringing. The street bowed and sprang beneath her. She had been afraid to call Gil because of the embarrassment, afraid to humiliate the boy in his moment of weakness, afraid of losing Gil's respect. Never afraid of this.

And how the memories came back to her. Peeking out the window as a child, seeing an elderly woman taken down the street in lockstep. The park, the teenage boys who annoyed a jogger's dog, and how the jogger locked the boys with his phone and marched them to the station. Playing the lockstep game, where if you were tagged you had to mimic the staggering walk. Whole afternoons like that, lurching around the park, competing with her friends to see who could do it best, groaning, slobbering, crossing her eyes, laughing so hard she collapsed in the clover.

They marched into a residential district where people were moving about, going to work, standing in line at the coffee shop, walking kids to school. The woman heard her own voice pleading with Gil and she sucked in her breath and made herself stop. It was too shameful. She tried to walk like a normal person. She realized that the boy, beside her, was moving quite easily, all emotion wiped from his face, almost as if entranced, as if, she thought miserably, he'd slipped back into a dream of his past, his cell, his chain. He held her arm, steadying her with a neutral, somnambulant touch.

Gil said something about Marjorie. They were going to Marjorie's place.

She clutched the boy's arm. "No," she said. "Gil. Not Marjorie."

"It's the closest place where there's somebody we can trust," snapped Gil. "Somebody from the scholarship committee. My God. Are you arguing with me?"

"Not Marjorie," said the woman, beginning to cry again. People on the street were looking at her, but she couldn't stop. The heat of shame swept through her, blistering. She thought of her colleagues. Her students. Her elders. Marjorie's blunt face and peevish eyes. She begged Gil to take off the lock. She couldn't bear to face Marjorie in lockstep.

"Do you hear yourself?" Gil demanded. "I have a class to teach this morning! What do you want me to do? Haul you to the station?"

"Just let us walk, we'll walk, we'll walk . . ."

He marched them into an apartment building. An elevator. He told her he was incredibly hurt. How could she have been so irresponsible, so childish? Did she want to set off an alert? Why had she run off with the boy, creating this embarrassing mess, then calling him at the crack of dawn?

"You know Rachel's mom has been sick. When the phone rang so early, she thought it was an emergency!"

The doors of the elevator opened. He marched them down a hall. He knocked at a door and stood shaking his head. "It just makes me feel like shit. That you didn't consider me at all. You didn't even think of me until you were in trouble."

Marjorie came to the door. Her face was oily with sleep and she pinched her robe at her throat. "What," she said.

"I'm so sorry," said Gil. "I need a favor."

Marjorie backed away so they could come through the doorway into the dim living room where plants and decorative objects stood on shelves. The boy and the woman stalked inside with the heavy swinging lockstep tread and the woman's leg crashed painfully into a table where something clattered.

"Watch out!" Marjorie yelped. "Those are heirlooms!"

"Shit. Sorry," said Gil.

He marched them to the wall, where embroidered pillows lay on the floor. "Sit down," he said. They sat clumsily, knees bent. The woman felt her ankleted foot pressed on the floor where some kind of fabric gleamed.

"Can they not step all over my throw?" Marjorie asked. "Because usually I ask my guests to leave their shoes at the door."

"Sorry," said Gil. He touched his phone and the woman's leg straightened instantly, yanked by the anklet, at the same time as the boy's. And while Gil explained what had happened, where he had found them, and what he wanted, the woman moved gingerly on the pillows to find a more comfortable position, eventually lying back against the wall. And now it had happened. She had been seen in lockstep by Marjorie, and she was here. And now that the awful moment had passed, or rather, was still going on, now that she was living inside the moment she had considered intolerable, she saw that she was tolerating it, lying against the wall in this fussy apartment that smelled of hand lotion and desiccated flowers. *What did*

I think? she wondered. *That time was going to end?* But time went on. She heard Gil's voice. She saw Marjorie's rounded shoulders and tight little bun of hair. "So I need you to take over," said Gil. "Can you do that?" And Marjorie said the whole thing was outrageous. "I just got up! I haven't even had coffee!"

Marjorie stumped into the kitchen, which was visible from the living room, separated only by a counter. She flicked on the light and banged open a coffee tin. The woman could see her scowling face bent over the stove while Gil leaned on the counter and remonstrated with her. The woman realized that she herself had not spoken to Marjorie, not one word of apology, self-justification, or even greeting, as if lockstep had placed her outside the social realm, in some shadow world of blue fire and paralysis. She turned to look at the boy.

"Are you all right?" she whispered.

He moved his head on the pillow with the trace of a smile. "Blueleg blueleg trim my sail," he murmured.

"What's that?"

"Just an old story. I didn't understand it till now. When I first saw you, I thought *you* were the blueleg witch."

"The blueleg witch?"

"Who takes your eyes and makes the whole world white. But it wasn't you, professor. It was them all the time."

Fresh tears filled her eyes. "I'm sorry," she whispered. "I shouldn't have called Dr. Gil. I should have listened to you."

He turned to look at her. And she felt, for the third time, through her anklet, even in its frozen state, his phantom touch. A feeling of reassurance.

"What is that?" she asked fearfully.

"Don't you ever try to reach out with the anklet? Say something?"

"No," she said. She tried to imagine what he meant. She thought about reaching through her anklet to say she'd changed her mind about everything, she was ready to go down any tunnel, try any scheme he had, because she was sick of her life, sick, and when she thought about all her days, the stream of hours she'd dedicated to things that now seemed unbearably stupid, all the meetings, the committees, the running from place to place, the concern, the late nights, the frantic messages flying back and forth, and for what, to change the "Department of the Old Knowledge" to the "Department of the Older Knowledge"—when she thought that she'd spent her time, her life, on *this*, when she remembered receiving the Unity Award, and how happy she'd been, standing on the stage with President Lyle, holding up that tacky little plaque while Gil called her the department's rising star, she wanted to smack herself in the face.

Her anklet surged. It glowed. She felt her energy meet the energy of the boy. His anklet had brightened too. She tried to move her foot.

No—she couldn't move it. *But I thought about it.* She knew it had crossed the boy's mind too. They looked at each other. *We thought about it.*

Marjorie came toward them with a tinkling tray and set it down between them. "Try not to spill anything," she said.

There were two cups of coffee and some rolls on the tray. The rolls were cold, with a musty fragrance, as though they'd been wrapped in scented tissues. The woman wolfed one down.

"We really don't have time for this," said Gil.

Marjorie faced him, her hands on her hips. "I think you have time for it. Since you've invaded my home with two people in lockstep, two people *I'm* apparently supposed to babysit for you, who should probably be in jail right now, I think you have time for it!"

"I said I was sorry." Gil rubbed his forehead. "God, I have such a headache! Will you take them or not?"

"Fine," said Marjorie. She picked up her phone from the counter and trained it on the woman and the boy. There was no change in the anklets as the lock moved to the new device.

"Have you got them?"

"Yeah."

"Okay. Shit, I'll have to call a cab."

He tapped at his phone, and Marjorie placed her phone down on the counter and sat on a stool beside it, blowing on her coffee, taking tiny sips and sometimes nibbling at a roll with her small, straight teeth. *She's enjoying the hell out of this,* the woman thought. Her anklet surged again, still connected to the boy. She registered, not his thought, but his feeling, his promise to stand with her against Marjorie's contempt. Then Gil approached, and she made her face a blank.

"I want you to know," said Gil in a tense, vibrating voice, "that I am devastated by this whole thing. I cannot believe that you of all people would jeopardize our work. Don't you know what will happen to the scholarship if you get sent down?" He waved his arms, his bracelet slipping and clicking against his cuff links. "It'll be over! Finished!" he shouted. "I've given ten years of my life to this. For you! For him!" He flung his arm toward the boy, who lay against the pillows, flat and still like some discarded thing. And the woman lay beneath the rush of Gil's anger in the same way. Gil said he had worked so hard. He had risked his position for the woman's sake. Didn't she know where they were? This was the Fleet! United Mining ran everything—approved every University program, every course, every textbook, practically every pen. And he had challenged them for her sake, for Unity and Multiplicity. He was changing the world so that people like her, ankleted people, could go to school. So that a boy from the Hold could study art and learn to express himself. And he, Gil, had suffered the consequences. He had been passed over for a promotion. "Did you know? Did you ever think to ask?" He had endured the mockery of his colleagues who thought he was a fool to mentor an ankleted colleague, let alone a chained boy. They had warned him—Alvin, Raymond, Marjorie (and here Marjorie nodded, self-satisfied, touching her tongue to her fingertips to remove a few grains of sugar)—they had warned him that the woman and the boy would never reward his efforts. "I didn't believe them. I thought we were friends. You came to my house. You played with my kids!"

He stopped and covered his eyes with his hands. He rubbed his face roughly and let out a brief, harsh cry of frustration. Then he leaned on the counter, gazing down at Marjorie's carpet, drumming his fingers a little, resting his other hand on his hip. "Okay," he said. "Okay. We can still fix this." And the woman found herself looking at him as if from a great distance, feeling that only the clamp of her anklet was holding her down in that apartment, hearing the words *if you get sent down*, the clang of them over and over, realizing that this much at least was true:

she might have been sent to the Hold.

"Do you want that?" Gil said, looking at her steadily. "Answer me."

She couldn't speak. She shook her head. Tears spilled out of her eyes. *No, no, I don't want to go down.* To the icy core of the Ship, where she would be chained, where she would lose everything: her friends, her students, her work. The thought of her research paper, that poor little stack of notes on her desk, with no one to care for it, no one to see it through to completion, struck her heart. *No, I don't want to go down.*

"Then you can't behave like this," said Gil. "And neither can he. Running all over the Ship without authorization! My God!"

He said he would need her solemn promise: no more unauthorized actions, no more disruptions from the boy. "You will call and check in with me every night. I am going to keep this program on track. I will not be humiliated. Oh, and that community engagement project— that's over. From now on, you stay upstairs."

A sob escaped the woman. She ducked and wiped her tears on her shoulder.

Gil sighed. "This is hard for me too," he said in a gentler tone. "This isn't how I want it to be, believe me. I'll come back after my class and pick you up, okay? We'll talk more then, when we've both had a chance to cool off."

His phone chimed. He thanked Marjorie and went out.

The woman finished the coffee. She could hear Marjorie grumbling to herself. She thought about what Gil had said and remembered the prophet lying quietly on his side in the icy core of the Ship. His breath a narrow thread. And she would never see him again, never hear his voice. The Hold was lost to her. Was this escape or exile?

A feeling disturbed her thoughts. A keen relief. She moved her leg. She could move her leg.

She looked up, and Marjorie was putting her phone down on the counter. Her face still corrugated with ill temper.

"Okay," Marjorie said. "That prick should be a mile off by now. What do you want me to do?"

3

The Chain

DR. MARJORIE WALKED WITH THEM down to the dock. She chatted with the pilot and handed him the letter she had written. She gave the professor a copy of the letter, said, "Don't lose it," and stood gruff and glowering under the bland dock lights. People were handing off their luggage, tugging at children, and entering the disinfection chambers in small groups. The pilot nodded toward a door. "Downstairs," he told the professor. "Enter through E Gate." And he turned to talk to another passenger.

"Okay," said Dr. Marjorie. "That's it. You're on your own."

"Wait," the professor said. She wanted to know, before Dr. Marjorie went—was it Dr. Marjorie who had called her "hard to work with and occasionally overbearing" in her last review? And Dr. Marjorie said yes, she had definitely written that, because the professor *was* overbearing and also a pain in the ass. And with that, Dr. Marjorie turned and left. And the boy and the professor entered the door of the lift and rode down to the Hold.

The Hold had its own dock. The boy had seen it only in the visions that drew him toward the child, never in waking life. A place of noise and terror. The guards shouted. The people cowered. The boy saw them peel off their singlets and stumble in their chains to a single disinfection chamber. There they were engulfed in a thick white fog. The boy was sent to a different chamber, the one for male guards. He had to strip and put all his clothes in a special box. Steam burst around him during the disinfection, and the ferry guards joked with him and made bets on whether he would throw up during the trip. And he could feel the distance like a chain. It was almost palpable, like a series of links he could trace with his outstretched hand. He felt the prophet in one direction and the child in the other, as if some part of him swung between them, suspended in midair.

On the far side of the chamber, he put on a suit and a helmet and heavy boots. The boots were too big for him, and the ferry guards laughed, the sound of it splintering through his helmet. Outside in the hall, the professor stood hesitant in her suit. Her eyes big behind the glass, her anklet tense inside her boot. The boy felt her reach for him and he met her gesture, establishing their connection. He told her, not knowing how much she understood, but knowing she felt his impulse, his will, that she should not be afraid, because he knew where he was, he knew where he was going, he stood between the prophet and his child, a conduit for the breath between them, and so he could not be lost. He kept on telling her this while they were strapped into their seats on the ferry, while a guard showed him the button on his suit that would suck vomit out of his helmet.

On the other side of a wall of mottled glass, he saw the chained. They were packed into the space on horizontal slats. Naked. Their bodies pressed to the glass. The whole space, from floor to ceiling, was crowded with bodies. He saw an eye. A scalp. The palm of a hand, golden and veined, a cracked lamp.

He could feel the professor strapped in beside him, burning. And when the ferry departed, with a terrible shudder and lift that made him retch, as the guards had predicted, he felt through his sickness the professor's grief and rage. She strained at the straps, shouting something the boy didn't understand. He heard the word *cocktails*. When the motion of the ferry eased, and a queasy lightness filled him, so that his gloved hands floated, he heard her more clearly, her voice crackling into his helmet.

"They're having cocktails upstairs. They're having a dance. They have gambling tables."

The guards laughed. "You're on the wrong detail. Did

you think this was food services?"

The boy closed his eyes. He breathed. He tried to link himself to everyone: the professor, the child, the guards, the people on the other side of the glass. But it was too much for him. He couldn't keep hold of all the connections. He let himself relax. *Start with one,* he thought.

He could hear the professor weeping. "The kneebone connected to the shoulderbone," she said wildly. "The anklebone connected to the neckbone."

The guards looked at each other in silence. One shrugged and fiddled with a glove. Another turned to look pensively at the glass.

The ferry docked on another Ship. The straps on the seat went *click* and slipped back into their grooves. The boy's body felt compact again, heavier than usual. He dragged his boots toward the door. He looked back to see what was happening to the people but a guard put a hand on his shoulder and made him step down.

After he was disinfected again and dressed in his clothes, which came out of their box freezing cold, with an acrid smell, he met the professor in a Hold just like his own: the same sloped floor, the same feeble lights on the walls. The professor looked glazed and wobbly but she spoke confidently to the foreign guard and unfolded her letter from Dr. Marjorie with a snap.

"It's been authorized upstairs," she said.

The guard looked doubtfully at the paper without touching it. "College program, huh," he said. "Okay, sis." He spoke with an odd accent, intelligible but mushy, as if he held a small object in his mouth.

They moved down the hall. The boy felt tingly, buoyant. As if on the ferry again. But no, he thought, that wasn't right, he didn't feel weightless at all, what he felt was tied, held, possessed by some force other than gravity that drew him like a current toward the child. It pulled him through the foreign Hold and up a metal ladder, just like the ladders on his own Ship, to the work level, where the air was alive with familiar noises: shouts and stamping, the whine of machines, and the far-off, juddering drone of the compost train. He thought of the other Ships of the Fleet, each of them shaped like this one. The same design. And for a moment his awareness extended beyond himself, entering the geometry of a series of rings so dizzyingly identical, he lost his balance and stumbled against the wall.

"Hey," said the professor, taking his arm.

The guard looked worried. "He all right?"

"Yes," the professor said, looking into the boy's face, sending a beam of consolation through her anklet.

"They're so many," he whispered.

"I know," she said. "But you know what you're doing, don't you? You know where to go."

The boy nodded and lurched upright. He still felt the foreign vessel spinning around him, a giddy mirror of his own Ship, both of them mirroring others that mirrored the circle of the blue anklet and the coarser, squatter, more abrasive shape of the bolt he'd worn most of his life. *A circle,* he thought, as they stopped at the door of the rock room, where the guard gave the boy and the professor little white masks. *A circle that hides the seat of the soul.*

Inside the rock room, dust clogged the air, and a gang of women stood bent over, chipping rock. And the child was there. She was just as he had seen her. Chained to her gang. Cracking rocks one-handed. *A soul,* he thought, *in the middle of a ring.* She was exactly as he had seen her. *The Hold is the soul of the Ship,* he thought. His chest ached. There was a roaring in his ears.

Through the roaring he could hear the sound of the hammers on the rock and the professor behind him asking the guard about the great pile of boulders, and through the chalky air he could see the women chipping, their skin and hair powdered with grit, their singlets ragged where they had torn off pieces to make themselves masks, and riding the wave of rogue gravity, of the Practice like an invisible chain, he went to the prophet's child and spoke to her, and when she looked at him, her eyes fringed with dust above the makeshift mask, he felt as if someone had tapped him on the heart.

"I'm here to take you back to your papa," he heard himself say.

The child was silent. He could not read her eyes through the veil of dust.

"I'm not a guard," he said. "I'm your papa's gangmate."

Her eyes widened. "You must be the green man," she said.

~

The child was slight, with bony shoulders and a scar on the bridge of her nose between the thick-lashed, searching eyes that gave her the look of the prophet, and she glanced back over her shoulder at the woman and the boy as she was led in chains to the disinfection chamber. Somehow—foolishly—the woman had expected to see a little child, but this girl, the prophet's daughter, appeared to be around the same age as the boy: the age, the woman thought, of the years the prophet had suffered her absence, the age and height and weight of a father's pain. She wondered if the prophet had been drawn to the boy in part because the boy was close to the age of his lost child. And looking at the boy, exchanging one swift glance of dazzled triumph before they separated for disinfection, she wondered if she herself had been drawn to him because of her own lost father, because he was like a fragment of her father's boyhood. These were links, she thought, as chemical cleansers gushed around her, that could not be scoured away, could not be purged.

She put on the suit and helmet. She entered the ferry and sat opposite the boy, sensing the jubilant fizzing of his anklet. He was like a spark, a fleck of fire held down by the straps of his seat, grinning helplessly behind the bowl of his helmet. *And let him enjoy it,* the woman thought, clenching her gloved hands as the ferry left the dock, *let him have this moment, and let me have it too,* closing her eyes on the lift and sickness, drawing strength from the boy, who, after all, had done something miraculous, who had plucked the child from the sunken coils of the Fleet, from the underground, as if drawing one diamond shard from the place of eternal winter.

The woman did not understand how this could be. *But here we are.* No matter what they faced on their return to the Ship—whether she managed, as she hoped, to keep her place at the University, calling on Marjorie to help her heal her breach with Gil, or whether, as her flinching mind still refused to fully imagine, she and the boy were chained forever in the Hold—here they were. The ferry entered its drifting stage, so that her body lightened as if filled with air. She opened her eyes in an effort to grasp where she was: right here, between two panes of glass, on one side the bright Fleet, on the other the stacked bodies of the chained. Turning her head slightly to the right she could see the stars; turning slightly to the left she could see the chained. *The humanization of space,* she thought. She could not see the child they had brought away with them in the crush behind the glass, where crates had been stored with the human cargo. Her heart veered, and she closed her eyes again, fighting vertigo, willing herself to stay calm, not to scream and cry as she had on the journey out, when the expansion of her world had seemed unbearable, the new information forcing a rearrangement of all she knew. The cruelty of this realization. The desolation of it. To know that the ferries to other Ships, which had always glittered for her with adventure and romance, were carrying, in addition to merry vacationers with their cocktails, this other and terrible freight, the people shunted to and fro like stones. To know that these people counted for so little that anyone holding a phone could intervene in their lives, as if ordering a meal to be delivered, could type and sign a quick letter authorizing the transfer of any chained person from one Ship to another, just as Marjorie had done.

She remembered the early morning, mere hours ago. Marjorie's scented apartment, Marjorie's heirloom china on the table, Marjorie's fingers jabbing at the keys of the computer on her kitchen counter with a hard, resentful efficiency. The curved bulwark of Marjorie's shoulders, her hunched, defensive stance. The way she drew in her cheeks, chewing them on the inside. Was this a kind of sorrow?

"Long ago," Marjorie said, "one of my ancestors started an insurance agency. Same one my father ran. My brother runs it now."

This agency, she said, covered damages to the Hold. In the last Great Move, when United Mining had jettisoned the Hold, Marjorie's ancestor, known as Big Tom, had had to pay the owners of the Hold so much to cover the loss, the agency had gone bankrupt.

"They called it an Act of God," Marjorie sneered. "Act of God! They knew they were going to do it. Otherwise the Ship would be too heavy to move. The tunnels down there, the cells, the chains, the cargo—it's too much weight." She described the legendary wrath of Big Tom, who called the owners and investors of the Hold a bunch of shits. He said it to their faces in the court. But he still lost everything. His house, the dogs, the pool his wife needed so badly to soothe her rheumatism. His little horse, Red Joe, that he loved to ride along the river. Everything but his china. He died in a council flat, surrounded by teapots.

"So I'm not doing this for you," said Marjorie, clicking PRINT. "I'm doing it for Big Tom. I don't know what you're up to, and I don't want to know, but I know you're against the Hold—you with your scholarships and community programs, going upstairs and down. You fooled Gil, but you can't fool me. You're against the Hold and the bastards that run it. That's all I need to know." She spoke of her family's struggles, the generations who had fought to rebuild the business. How they had tried to shift into other areas, diversify, make safer bets, but there wasn't any space, the other agencies blocked them, nobody would give them a single break and their contacts were still with the Hold and from sheer desperation they wound up underwriting the new Hold as it was built.

"And I know," said Marjorie, taking the sheets from the printer and signing her name to the two copies, "that the next time it happens, we'll go down again. And those assholes who are already raking in government money for running the Hold, who get paid for every bolt and chain in that damn place—they're going to screw us again." She folded the letters neatly into thirds, pressing the folds with her thumbnail. "So if you can screw *them*? Do it."

The woman swallowed. She glanced at the boy, who sat cross-legged on the carpet, dunking a roll in coffee. "But they won't jettison the Hold again," she said. "It was necessary at the time, but not now. We have advanced fusion drives now, more efficient—"

Marjorie gave a hard laugh. "Are you kidding me?"

She looked at the woman pityingly from under her

rugged brows. (On the ferry, the woman remembered that look. Its deep coldness, penetration, and certainty.) "And you have a PhD," Marjorie said. "I swear, they'll give anybody a degree these days. Look, the Hold is a *business,* get it? These people don't invent shit unless it makes money. Sure, there's all kinds of advertising about advanced drives and whatnot, to court investors. But when the next Great Move comes, the question will be: What's cheaper? And trying to move a heavy Ship with a core full of concrete and iron will never be cheaper. Never. It's a matter of numbers."

"But then what's it for?" the woman asked. "Why have a Hold at all?"

"You poor sap," said Marjorie. "Didn't you hear me? *Money.*" She pressed the heel of her hand to her brow. "God, you people in the Old Knowledge are so slow. Making cute presentations about kids jumping rope in the street." She dropped her hand and looked at the woman. "Yeah, I went to your presentation. You didn't see me? Weak stuff, in my opinion. Obvious. Shallow. But your buddy Gil was eating it up with a spoon. If you hadn't pulled this stunt today, he probably would've nominated you for another award. Look, this is simple, okay? Certain things are always with us." She counted on her fingers. "One: scarcity. Limited space and resources. Two: the need to maintain order, which, when things are scarce, is always under threat. Three: surplus. Too many people, not enough stuff: the result is extra people. What are you going to do with all these extra people? If you're smart, you'll turn them into a business. That's the Hold. So there will always be a Hold. Because the Ship is a problem. And the Hold is the answer."

On the ferry the woman remembered Marjorie's words, their acid logic. Nausea filled her throat. To steady herself, she murmured phrases from her own research paper, bracing herself on the well-known words as if touching the glow of her anklet. "The 'nowhere games' of ankleted children illustrate informal design, understood as a lively immersion in the potential of abandoned things." The child, the child, abandoned, neglected, cast off. "In the game of Pick," the woman whispered, "a child can delineate a palace, a river, a Ship, or any other structure the child names, based on the arc a small flung object describes in the air." And she was a small flung object in the air. And the child was too, and the boy, and the prophet, and all the chained. And who named the structure, who got to pick?

She looked at the boy strapped into his seat across from her, gazing raptly out the window, stars reflected in his helmet's curve. He seemed inordinately precious to her, with this gift that, she knew, he had imparted to her on some level, revealing a new way to use the anklets, a gift that was therefore hers as well but also much larger than she could grasp: the web, the whorl, the wheels within wheels, the Practice.

She knew so little about it. She could not even say whether it belonged to the Older or Newer Knowledge, whether it partook of both, or whether it was of a different kind, alien to the question of old or new, unfurling itself outside the terms, an outside knowledge. Tentatively she reached out through her anklet toward the boy, as if groping in shadows. At once he turned to face her, beaming. She remembered him sitting on the rim of a hole in a dark warehouse, jittery with his new force. *I made this shape. And now it's making me.*

She knew they were going back to a hostile Ship. *But it was always a hostile Ship,* she thought.

She looked to the left, at the heavy glass that imprisoned the chained, glass that would never break though the people strained against it with all their force, its surface scratched by the thrust of their bones and blurred with their breath. She turned her head. The ferry dipped. They were coming into the dock. She gritted her teeth at the sudden weight of her flesh, the return. While the Fleet stretched out around her, the asteroids with their powdery glow, and the countless, burning, ever-receding stars.

Limited space? she thought.

~

You must be the green man.

On the way back to the Ship where he had been born the boy thought of the child, concentrating through the glass that separated them, maintaining a link with her presence, feeling her panic in the black, stifling compartment, her gasp as the gravity released. He kept hold of the small flame of her all through the ordeal of disinfection, and when he found her waiting outside the chamber, clad in a singlet, separate from the others, a guard clasping her chain, his chest constricted with raw joy. Her lips had a dry whiteness and she tottered where she stood, but she looked at him the same way as before: grave, trusting, intent. He moved toward her, and the guard—one the boy knew, the same one who oversaw his meetings with the prophet—nodded to him and passed him the length of chain. The boy stood holding the child's chain in the chaos of the dock, in the clatter of ferry ramps, the sound of moans, the yelling of the guards. Her gaze a solemn darkness. He wanted to speak, but he noticed the professor arguing with the guard, waving the paper from Dr. Marjorie in the air.

"You know I want to help you out," said the guard, his hands open, placating. "Haven't I been helping you all along? But there's an alert on you. I have to respect the alert, don't I? So why don't I take you up to the Warden, and you can show *him* that letter."

"This is an authorized project!" the professor shouted. The boy felt her reach out, frantic, through the sizzle of the anklets.

He joined his energy seamlessly to hers and directed the sparkling flow toward the guard, easily, gently, knowing now how to touch without startling. The guard paused in his argument, then glanced between the professor and the boy, unsure what was happening, feeling just a faint vibration at first, and then, slowly, a growing sense that others were calling him, a subtle tightening of the skin beneath his anklet.

There was no command. Only a call. The boy felt his connection not only to the guard and the professor, but to the child and the prophet down in his cell. The prophet's breath a shadow, the child's strong, unflagging, willful. The boy felt the currents meet and swell. The guard sighed.

"I'll set you up with the old man. But then I'll have to fetch the Warden. There's an alert on you."

The professor thanked him almost in a whisper. The boy felt her holding herself together as she stalked after the guard, her movements stiff and abrupt. He felt her trying not to run. He saw, through her eyes, the darkness of the long corridor, like a great throat swallowing them, he felt her blank unyielding terror of the Hold, and walking behind with the child he tried to send the professor ease, to settle her heart, which had been shocked by the word *alert*. That word had frightened him, too. But the child was at his side, and he could not look at her without a thrill like a flame between his ribs. She was trailing her fingers along the coarse, stained, ill-lit wall, the same as the walls of the Hold on the other Ship.

"Is this where I was born?" she whispered.

"Yes," said the boy. "This is your papa's Ship." He swallowed. "What did you mean about the green man?"

A glance from the edge of her gleaming eye. "It was a dream," she said in a hushed voice. She had dreamed of a man. He was tall, so tall his head scraped the top of the Hold. He had a great thin face that was full of sadness and his beard hung down in greenish rags like the mold that sometimes grew along the pipes. "I thought he was a moldy man and I wanted to move away from him but could not." He crouched beside her, carrying sadness in his face, sadness in his eyes that were brimful, as if, should he tip his massive head, grief would come spilling out. She saw that he had a white bag on a strap over his shoulder. "It was his bag of cures," she told the boy. "It was all made of bone." The body of the bag was formed from shoulder blades clamped together and it opened with a zipper of human teeth. The green man moved very slowly, in the manner of creeping mold, and opened the bag. He took something out of it and placed it in the child's palm, something white that shimmered in the dark. She thought it was a little fingerbone, until it moved, and she saw it was a grub.

"And you think I'm the green man?" asked the boy.

"I don't know. I just said that." Light danced at the corner of her eye. He noticed she was trembling. She held her sore hand close to her body. "I don't know anything. But the man came out of nowhere, and he was strange. Just like you."

A clash of metal: the guard was opening the door of one of the Meet Rooms. He said it was the only place where he could put different sexes together. He took the child's chain from the boy in an indifferent, routine gesture, locked it to the wall, and went to collect the prophet.

In the bare room, much like the other cells, but with no sign of human habitation, no jumbles of castoff or pictures scratched on the walls, the boy and the professor sank to the floor beside the child, and the professor touched both of their faces, laughing and crying. "Here we are. Here we are," she said. The boy felt the spread of the Practice. He sensed the mesh. It was no longer something outside himself that he strove to enter through drawings on walls or paper. He remembered his trip out on the ferry, such a short and long time ago, when he had tried to hold many connections at once, and failed. But now it was as if he flexed some new or newly activated muscle. He gathered the threads lightly, as if in a game, tracing them with his breath as if strumming fibers with his fingers: the child, the professor, the guard who was leading the prophet down the hall. *Maybe I really am the green man,* he thought, and he remembered how his friends at school had called him Fluke, and it made him laugh, because he was so ordinary and yet so strange, an ordinary boy who had made himself strange through a Practice so simple anyone could take it up, because everybody breathes. He remembered how the thought of the changeless repetitive lines of the Fleet had filled him with dread, and that made him laugh harder, because it was sameness that made the Practice, it was repetition that kindled the power of breath, and it was the changeless stuff of all things that fashioned the bonds in the endless chain.

The child asked why he was laughing and he told her, "Here I went all this way to fetch you and you called me a moldy man."

She covered her mouth, her eyes bright. "I didn't mean it like that," she protested.

"I know," said the boy, still laughing. "But never mind that now. We have to take care of your hand."

The child did not ask how he knew she was hurt. He told the professor about her injury, and the professor tore the lining out of her jacket and bound the child's hand and wrist. The child was twitching the tips of her fingers experimentally when the guard led the prophet into the room.

The prophet stumbled a little, his eyes misting over.

"Come on," said the guard, pulling the chain. He locked the prophet to the wall beside the child. He spoke to the professor as he replaced the big key in his pocket, telling her something the boy couldn't understand— faded, unnecessary words. What the boy saw was the prophet squatting carefully by the wall, not touching the child, his face broken by a tender smile. The child stared, then slowly reached to touch the old man's cheek. And the boy realized that he had found the River that was a Sea.

~

The woman sat on the floor with the others, watching the child, who stroked the prophet's cheek with a hesitant finger, then cupped his face in her hands. The prophet put his own hands softly over the hands of the child, touching her skin and the bandage the woman had made from the lining of her jacket. The woman closed her eyes.

She could feel her heartbeat. She heard the prophet whisper that even the oldest bones could knit again. "These old dry bones," he said. And the child whispered, "I had a dream about all this. A dream about a green man."

Her voice was hoarse, ecstatic. She babbled, recounting a dream of a green stranger who came to her with a living creature in his bag of bone. "A little grub. It had one wing in the middle of its back. I said, 'How is it going to fly with just one wing?'"

If only we could stay inside this space, the woman thought. But the guard had gone away to fetch the Warden. And even as the prophet spoke, in that slippery singing accent the woman found hard to follow, so that she could only tell he was speaking about wings, about wings joined one to another and living creatures whose appearance was as a lamp, the woman heard the tramp of returning boots.

She opened her eyes as the guard entered the room. He stood to one side, his feet shifting, his eyes cast down. Behind him was Gil.

Of course, the woman thought.

Of course, when the guard had gone to fetch the Warden, it was not the Warden who had come to find them, it was Gil, for Gil, of course, was looking for them, it was he who had set the alert to watch for them, for her in particular: his colleague, his friend, his—what? *What am I to you?* she wondered, standing up to face him, observing his sweating brow, his outstretched hand clutching his phone, his sharply cut hair and impeccably shaven jaw and trim white shirt incongruous against the rough walls of the room. He held one sleeve before his face, his eyes watering in the foul air, his bracelet jingling. *What am I?* She saw herself for a moment through his eyes: the unkempt hair, the hollow cheeks, the torn and crumpled clothes, the sullen stance. Then his thumb twitched, and the vise closed on her leg.

Lockstep. But it was not for the first time. He made her jerk forward, separating her from the others. She staggered, rigid, unweeping, obeying the cruel command of the lock but not lowering her gaze, her eyes fixed on Gil with a dry ferocious glare.

He panted behind his sleeve. When he shook his head, his bracelet clinked. "Look at you. What would your father say?"

And suddenly she did not care what she was to him at all.

"Don't you dare talk about my father," she said.

Gil paled. But she saw that he knew he had gotten through to her, and he pressed his advantage. "What would he say, after all his efforts to give you a better life, if he knew you'd thrown everything away to come back down here? Because that's what's going to happen, unless you let me help you. You'll be down here. Chained!"

"Don't you talk about him!" she shouted. Her anklet writhing, burning.

He said she had one chance. She would have to give up the boy, the prophet, and the Hold. "It's your own fault. You did this. You have destroyed the scholarship program." Now, he said, the best she could hope for was to stay upstairs. She would write personal apologies to Marjorie, the Dean, the Provost, and the Board—"and me," he added bitterly, "if you think it matters." He told her he was her only chance to survive. That it would take all his prudence and skill. He'd have to fight for her, call in favors, because after threatening Marjorie with a kitchen knife (and she almost laughed through her rage and the gathering fire), after holding a knife to Marjorie's ribs and forcing her to write that letter, the woman would have the whole population of the Ship screaming for her blood (and no, she thought, not the whole population, only the ones upstairs, not the many below, the God knows how many below, unreckoned unheard unrecorded unknown, consigned to a life of terror and meaningless labor that could have been done by machines, scraping at floors and chipping at stones out of sight out of mind in the dawnless dark), and only he, said Gil, only he could help her now, "and you're coming upstairs," he said, "to think about this, because you're not thinking clearly right now, because if you were, you'd have some respect for the *years* I've put into mentoring you, not to mention your father's—"

"Don't talk about him! You don't even know his name!"

Gil paused.

"Don't you dare talk about him unless you say his name."

The fire seemed to come up through the floor. It seemed to come down through the ceiling. It came through the walls. It came from every direction, invisible and yet blue. Imperceptible to the eye and yet blue in her mind, it came from the boy, it came from the guard in his secrecy silently cheering for her in the corner, it plunged through her body and fanned out like a wave, she felt it upstairs, suddenly she saw the jaded elder in her apron at the stove, saw her in crisp and lucid detail and heard her speak to the humble elder, who sat at the kitchen table, they were talking about Gil, how he had come to ask them about the woman and the boy. She could hear the jaded elder's spoon in the pan. She smelled the frying onions. *Can the University be a place of both training and transformation?* she thought, and tears pricked her eyes as she answered, *No. No, because it's not possible to do both of those things at once.* But then she thought of the boy, the prophet, and the Practice. Wasn't the Practice a form of training—something the prophet had taught the boy, something the boy had worked on all his life? Was it training—was it not training—when children met in the barren neglected streets and immersed themselves for hours in a game of Scatter? Searching, testing, repeating again and again the attempts on the goal, seeking the singular instant when the arcs coincided, the ball meeting head or foot, when the collision passionately desired and designed occurred at last, with a whiplike grace that belied the evenings of sweat and shouting that made it possible. Hadn't the boy trained the woman, in his way? So that now she skimmed through the jaded elder's kitchen like a shaft of light. She heard the scornful, beloved voice.

"Dr. Gil! I never liked him. With his pointy head."

"Hush," said the humble elder, shaking with soundless laughter.

Perhaps there were forms of training she did not know. Disciplines as yet unrecognized by her elders, her father, or herself. She saw the two elders suddenly start and look at each other and knew they felt her touch, her call. Their energy shot toward her.

She took a step.

She took a single unbidden, forbidden step.

Gil stared at her. He looked at his phone and shook it and looked at her again. She thought of her father upstairs, in the evenings, sipping at what he loved most: water. The one thing that still connected him to the Hold.

"Say. His. Name!"

She dragged her foot forward again. A warped, unlovely motion. As if pulling it through deep mud. But it moved.

"I—" Gil said, and looked at the guard. "What's happening?"

The guard raised both hands in a gesture of amazement and ignorance. Unseen, his energy streaked toward her.

The woman took a third step. Blue light coursed into her and out again, so that she was a node, a joint, like one of the dark spots in the boy's drawings. She pushed the light fiercely against the lock on her ankle. Gil blinked at her. A shudder went through him, violently shaking the hand that held the phone. For an instant the woman was seized by wonder: Was she affecting the phone? Was it possible to press, through the anklets, on those inaccessible instruments? Would there ever be a way to reach Marjorie again—Marjorie, who had denounced the woman to save herself, but whose hatred for United Mining might still make her a source of help? The thought flashed past, subsumed in the flood that filled her and overflowed and grew so that she could feel it tumbling out beyond the walls of the Ship, washing against the foreign vessels of the Fleet, rippling toward others like her, who looked up, confused for a moment in their dingy rooms, the ones she had never met at the conferences she had never attended but might touch otherwise, lightly now, playfully.

"What is this?" Gil whispered.

And she was a child again, in the park. Playing at lock-step. Lunging. Cross-eyed. *This is the zombie of your nightmares.* She swung toward him in a parody of captivity that was no captivity now, and he backed toward the door, trying to grip the phone with both hands, and he dropped the phone and they heard it smash on the floor. And the woman was unlocked. And Gil, her old friend, her old colleague, turned and fled.

~

Held. He was held in the web. In the net of the living and the dead. It illuminated his vision, pulsing, unfading, its contours folding him close. There was no struggle or doubt, but rather an increase of freshness and vigor with every breath, for he was inside it now and errant no more. And as people moved about him he felt them woven into the mesh, he sensed them like darting rays, felt the professor's triumph over the lock, the astounded exultation of the guard, who whooped and shouted and punched the air and ran up to grasp the professor's hand in both of his. "Who are you?" the guard cried, and the professor laughed and said they were a Scatter team, she and the boy and the prophet and the child, they were building up to the biggest game of Scatter ever played, a real nowhere game, and did the guard want to join them, and the guard said, "Hell yes."

The boy felt the guard's heart knocking as he unlocked the chains from the wall and he felt the chime of metal on metal spread like waves in a pool of water. He could feel the bright knot of life that was the child. The sinuous breath of the prophet gathering force as the old man got to his feet beside the wall. "Lock us together," the prophet told the guard, and the guard locked the prophet to the child, and the boy stood up and took the prophet's hand, knowing the child and the prophet still needed this pull, the weight and tension of the links. "But you will not need it always," he told the prophet.

"That may be," the prophet said, and he held the boy's hand tight in his callused grip, his eyes vivid in the dimness with something more than gratitude, a new pulse of resolution beating up from him, charging the web, a strength in contrast to the frailty of his bones.

Then a tug as the child moved suddenly and bent to the fallen phone, the fractured bits of glitter on the floor. The boy felt her curiosity, her eagerness as she tucked the phone into her singlet, retrieving each shard of glass and tying them up in her hem. *And I would be your green man and traverse your dream once more.* Suddenly sorrow pierced him: a jagged, unforeseen grief for his lost youth, for what should have been, for how he would have liked to meet the child, carelessly, in some open place, without burden and without fear. He saw her laughing in a thin dream-hour. In a light like froth, the gauzy atmosphere of a moment that had never come to pass, where he himself was entirely different, easy in his skin, unhurried, telling some story from an unknown life. He realized that this flash of a dream had come to him from the child her-self. He held to it, clutched it, drawing on it as an anti-dote to the sorrow, fortifying himself against despair with the shrewd and restless intelligence of the child, who in-tended, he knew, to live. That was why she had saved the phone and why she was talking with the others now, they had to move, she said, the force of her braced hard against the chain, the torque of her in the bounding web, and the guard led them down a hall, the child and the prophet and the boy following in a string. Last of all came the pro-fessor. *Start with one.*

The boy reached for her hand. He thought he had started with the child, but no, he had started with the professor. Or no, perhaps further back, he had started with the unfamiliar girl who had stood in Dr. Alvin's class, chained to the wall. Or no, he had begun with the mute bodies of the drowned. Or with the prophet. His mother's face in the distance like a fleck of light. How long was the chain? He did not know, and the not-knowing was no longer a source of dread but of expansive comfort and strength.

They crouched together in a dark place. He could feel metal pipes against the back of his head. The breath of the others close and steady in the gloom. Only the gleam of the anklets flickering softly against bare flesh, and he would warm himself, he thought, at the small blue light. And he would trim no witch's sail. And he would not rise up. He would go out. Out where the child was leading him, toward the dappled future light, out where the professor linked him into the blazing aquamarine that contained the guard and the elders and all his friends from school with their dances and loves, out where the prophet drew him with the measured humming practiced breath to the chained, not only the chained in this Hold but the chained in all the Ships of the Fleet and more, to the dead, to the myriad dead, for he felt the prophet quivering on the threshold of the otherworld and the thought of it opened a hole in his chest, a gaping hollow of woe through which he breathed and in which he breathed and burned and lived. The drowned were turning. With their eternally open mouths. They were turning with their stripped limbs in the water and in the air and the prophet knew them, touched them. The prophet was there to shepherd the boy in pain. Breathe, the prophet told him, and he breathed. And the drowned were looking at him from the waters of old Earth. And they were looking at him from the Hold. They were looking at him from the Holds of the ancient Ships, those cages cast into space without anchor, left behind by the Ships that departed in wheels of fire. He felt the ones who were left behind without air. In water. In space. In the Star called Wormwood. The killing breathlessness. But we are still alive. He remembered the guard telling him *You'll be a man of iron one day* and he felt the points in the body of the Ship that matched those in his own flesh. It made him glow all through his skin. The web extended throughout the Fleet, through stone and slag, through dirt and leaf and fur and milk and water, electric, coiling, hard as diamond, pliable as flesh, impressible and fluid, gathering in waves. He did not know what would happen if he dared to pull this chain. Would the force of it shock the phones to death? Would the anklets burn to smoke? Would the chains tear loose, would the Ships' floors crack, would the Holds spring out, would the dead come forth, he didn't know, couldn't know, couldn't predict, the mesh so dense he could barely see, but each of his hands was held by someone and one is where to begin to be, so watch now the bones as they knit and the wings that unfold in their luminosity, each new-hatched grub reaching delicately, finding others, first one, then two, then three, forming shapes of marvelous intricacy, of dazzling reach and vibrancy, through the bonds that link themselves endlessly, chaining you to the dead, to the living, to me, for

One is a River.

Everyone is a Sea.

~

The woman breathed the boy's name in the dark.

He opened his eyes. In the frail radiance of the anklets, she caught his turning gaze. She felt his energy, a bloom of light. The anklets brightened. How easily now, together, they poured out through the Fleet. She held the hands of the boy and the guard, she felt the child and the prophet, the closeness of their circle, crammed here in a corner of the Ship, and she felt the wider circle, the web, tensile, like a surface, growing ever more insistent in its force.

Light enveloped them. A pure, indigo incandescence.

No depth, she thought, smiling, trembling, clasping the hands of the others. *Breadth,* she thought. *Breath.*

"What do we do now?" she whispered.

The boy raised his chin. "Now," he said, "we pull."

The Practice, the Horizon, and the Chain

Sofia Samatar

Acknowledgments

The Practice, the Horizon, and the Chain was inspired by conversations at the virtual conference Building the Fugitive Academy: Communication, Culture, Media, and Rhetoric Scholars on the Work of Transformation, hosted by Boston College in 2021. I would like to thank the organizers—Aymar Jean Christian, Vox Jo Hsu, Sarah J. Jackson, Robert Mejia, Anamik Saha, and Anjali Vats—for the opportunities for thought and exchange they provided during that event. Special thanks go to my friend and former student Rayheem Eskridge, who attended the conference with me, and Myra Washington, whose presentation offered a refreshingly real and pragmatic approach to diversity work in higher education.

Both that conference and this novella were shaped by Stefano Harney and Fred Moten's *The Undercommons: Fugitive Planning and Black Study.* Thanks to Harney and Moten for the invitation of that book, especially the chapter "Fantasy in the Hold." Thanks to Christina Sharpe for the meditations and improvisations on the hold and the ship in *In the Wake: On Blackness and Being,* and to Dionne Brand for the spatial thinking of *A Map to the Door of No Return: Notes to Belonging.* Thanks also to all the students who have read these books with me.

Finally, my thanks to Aaron Bady and K'eguro Macharia for the generous insights; to my agent, Sally Harding, and my editor, Eli Goldman, for the careful attention and support; and to Keith Miller, my first reader.

About the Author

Jim C. Hines

SOFIA SAMATAR's first novel, *A Stranger in Olondria,* won the 2014 William L. Crawford Fantasy Award, the British Fantasy Award, and the World Fantasy Award for Best Novel, and was included in *Time* magazine's list of the 100 Best Fantasy Books of All Time. She also received the 2014 Astounding Award for Best New Writer. Her novel *The Winged Histories* completed the Olondria duology, and was followed by *Tender: Stories, Monster Portraits* (with the artist Del Samatar), and *The White Mosque: A Memoir,* a PEN/Jean Stein Award finalist. Samatar lives in Virginia and teaches at James Madison University.

TOR·COM

Science fiction. Fantasy. The universe.

And related subjects.

*

More than just a publisher's website, *Tor.com*
is a venue for **original fiction, comics,** and
discussion of the entire field of SF and fantasy,
in all media and from all sources. Visit our site
today—and join the conversation yourself.